DEVIL'S ARCADE-MAX PLANK 3

A MAX PLANK NOVEL

ROBERT BUCCHIANERI

Editing: Clicking Keys

❀ Created with Vellum

ALSO BY ROBERT BUCCHIANERI

Stray Cat Blues (Max Plank 1)
The Ties That Bind (Max Plank 2)
Mystery Thriller Triple Pack
Between a Smile and a Tear
Ransom Dreams
Butcher's Moon
Love Stings

For Buddy
A faithful and loyal friend

ONE

"Disappeared?" I said, then took a sip of the strong, black coffee, undoubtedly a French or Italian roast, from the gold-rimmed Wedgwood cup.

There's no way not to feel prissy when the tips of your fingers are struggling to hold onto a tiny curlicued handle. I prefer a plain solid mug, but I didn't complain. Coffee is coffee, and that morning, like most, I craved the buzz.

Poe nodded. His eyes, normally quick and alert like a fox's, reflecting a surprising note of sorrow or perhaps resignation.

With his short, trim build and his well-tended hair and goatee, along with his typical uniform of Italian-made Battistoni long-sleeved white shirt and black vest, he looked as smooth and suave as ever. But there was a distracted, preoccupied air to his manner, in place of the usual formidable intensity.

I looked away, angling my head toward the glass wall to the west, past Alcatraz, the abandoned prison rock, and out to the Golden Gate Bridge and its gleaming burnt-red spires, and the Gulf of the Farallones beyond which led eventually to Hawaii itself, which I was picturing in my mind.

In particular, my focus was on the hike down Waimea Canyon where I'd promised to lead Alexandra. I'd told her of the glories at the bottom of the canyon, the river and the waterfalls and the flowering plants and fruit trees. I could almost taste the strawberry guavas I'd sampled the last time I'd hiked down ten years before.

Alexandra had never been to Hawaii and I, relatively flush for the time being due to a recent case where I discovered the location of a lost lockbox for a client with more money than sense, had two round-trip tickets to Honolulu airport booked for the coming weekend.

I wanted to take Alexandra away. I had been a little neglectful in recent weeks, of her and our semi-adopted daughter, Frankie, and I felt guilty about it. She hadn't brought it up, but it bothered her.

She'd agreed to go with me, but it had been a big hassle for her to arrange the time away from her investigative work as a photojournalist. She'd also wanted to take Frankie along, but, as much as I care for the little girl, I thought a week alone was just what we needed.

Or maybe I'm just a selfish prick at heart.

Alexandra adored me, I'd assumed. And the relative coldness toward me recently didn't feel good. Which surprised me. My time with Alexandra is the longest relationship with a woman I've ever had, save for Mom. Normally by now, over three years in the big muddy, either me or the woman has long since bailed.

I care for her. I love her, whatever that means. I'd even told her, for what it's worth. She'd been telling me she loved me for more than a year before I finally offered the word up to her a couple of months ago. I hadn't repeated it since then, but she knew. She also knew I'd never used that word with any other woman, even my mother, if you don't count Mary Mathieson in the second grade at Our Lady of Mercy.

Mary giggled when I told her how I felt and scurried off to confer with her equally giggly friends.

I almost never got over it.

Alexandra seemed bothered that she was the first woman I'd told that I loved since I'd achieved puberty, roughly thirty years. I don't know why it irked her. I don't pretend to comprehend what lurks in the hearts and minds of women. That alone sounds sexist. Women are humans. Ordinary people. Just like men.

Right.

Anyway, Meiying and Dao had agreed to take care of Frankie for a week, and I would let nothing impede the trip, even and especially Poe's cry for help. I'd told him I'd listen to his story, but that was all.

"What does 'disappeared' mean?" I asked, biding my time.

He scratched his goatee, considering what to tell me. Behind him on an antique walnut desk was a large bust of Edgar Allan Poe, his hero, next to volumes of the master's works. The wall behind the desk was covered with framed posters of B-movies directed by Roger Corman and starring Vincent Price—*The Pit and the Pendulum, The Fall of the House of Usher, The Raven*—all adaptations of Poe's stories.

The room appeared that of an academic, a man a little obsessed by his subject. Poe had a master's degree in English literature. His thesis had been on some arcane aspect of Edgar's influence on modern-day horror writers.

All a tad surprising considering we were on the mysterious thirteenth floor of Pirate's Cove, a sprawling, octopus-shaped steel and glass casino and resort hotel on Treasure Island, an artificial heptagon-shaped spit of land, connected to a real island, Yerba Buena, which sits below the Bay Bridge, the Golden Gate's younger, but less attractive, sister connecting Oakland to San Francisco.

Even more surprising is the fact that Poe himself owns and

operates the casino complex, the public face of an empire with deep criminal roots in the San Francisco underworld.

The former academic has come a long way from his small-town east coast roots, and the story of that journey is cloaked in mystery. Nobody seems to know what really happened on his trek westward, and the couple of local reporters who've attempted to retrace Poe's steps have mostly ended up with more questions than answers. Most of the people who knew Poe well then have little or nothing to say about him now.

Poe talked slowly, carefully parsing his words. "Bobby's been working for me here for the past couple of years. I had him doing security work at first, some public relations too." He paused, stroking that perfectly manicured goatee again, shaking his head. "He'd had some problems. Never really found his place in the world."

Poe's younger sibling was nothing like his big brother. Actually, he was a larger man. Poe himself is trim but muscular. Bobby is taller but round-shaped with a big belly. He's kind of a mess. A boyish man who's never outgrown his adolescent awkwardness. He was eager to please his older brother who was clearly embarrassed by him. I couldn't believe that he was a blood relation to Poe, a dangerous man with a highly civilized veneer. Bobby was soft, kind-hearted, but kind of hapless. He loved dogs and *Star Trek* and was near helpless around women he was attracted to.

Poe was uncomfortable talking about Bobby. He wasn't exactly a touchy-feely kind of guy, but Bobby was his brother.

"He used to have a coke habit. It got pretty bad. He lost his wife because of it. Not that she was any prize." Poe shook his head, frowned. "She took him for all he had and some of what I have. Anyway, I got him in rehab and offered him the job here as long as he stayed away from the junk. I knew he smoked pot, but he said it helped him stay off blow."

It surprised me to hear that Bobby had a wife. It seemed altogether too adult and mature for the man. And then I remembered the countless masses—young, passionate, dumb, broke, unformed, yet pierced by Cupid's arrow, or Darwin's imperative, marching ceaselessly down the aisle, playing their part in the great game, and I wondered at my surprise. I hoped there were no kids involved but didn't interrupt Poe to ask. I wanted to hear him out, then turn his request down, and get back on track for Alexandra and Hawaii.

"...he was trying. He had a little knack for writing press releases, thank god, because otherwise, he wasn't earning his keep. But he's family. And I doubted he could find decent work elsewhere..."

Poe revealing a morsel of a heart I didn't know he had.

"... and then we got cheated. More than a million dollars now. Perhaps more. I noticed something different about it right away—"

"I haven't read about any of this."

He smiled, shook his head.

"You didn't report it."

"I take care of my own business."

"And you want no one shoving their curious noses into smelly corners of this place. I still don't know how you finesse the Bureau." The state Bureau of Gambling, the regulatory body that polices casino operations in our Golden State.

I also thought he wanted no one to know that he was a sucker of any sort and intended to deal with the culprits in a slightly more direct and decisive way than what the judicial system offered. But it looked like that hadn't worked out. Ergo, my presence here.

"We dot our i's and cross our t's. This is a completely law-abiding business that pays the city and state substantial tax revenues."

Pirate's Cove was an unusual hybrid. Only federally recognized Indian tribes may have casinos under California law, but Poe had engineered a strange, subtle partnership with the Arapahoe Indians to help secure a license. Indian tribes rarely pay taxes on gambling revenue, but in exchange for granting him the ability to print money, Poe had agreed to pay both local and state taxes.

I couldn't imagine the hundred-ton tub of green-tinged lard he must have used to grease the palms of both Indian and government bureaucrats to get the deal done.

I imagine everybody involved considered it a win-win.

"You're still a cynical bastard, Plank."

"Yeah. So did you find out who was stealing from you?"

"Not yet. It's only a matter of time though." Poe rose, walked over to the glass wall overlooking the bay. Outside, there was a bright, midday sun and a semi-blue sky, unfurling into a hazy forever sky.

He stood there with his hands on his hips for a long while then reached down and effortlessly touched his toes, dipped further into the forward bend, his palms flat on the floor, his knees locked straight.

He was flexible. So was I. We were both to be commended.

Poe re-assumed his full verticality and tapped his knuckles against the glass wall. "I think my brother was somehow involved in the conspiracy. His disappearance is related. I don't think he knew what was going on. They used him." He stopped, smacked the glass with his hands. "They must know who they're dealing with and yet they dared violate me. I'm perplexed."

He turned to face me, his facial muscles tightening over his bones, his eyes searching for an answer in my own.

I shook off his gaze and said, "What do you want from me?"

"I want you to find my brother."

"Have you looked for him?"

He nodded. "Yes. We've checked everywhere he might be, all of his favorite haunts. Art and Rex have scoured the Bay Area. We've examined his computer, contacted everyone he knows. Gotten nowhere."

"And, if you want me to find him, why are you telling me about the thefts?"

"Because when you find him, I believe you'll find the thieves."

"How can you be sure?"

He walked back to the formidable desk and picked up his phone and waited, his eyes skipping around the room, until I heard a female voice say hello.

"Angelique, would you mind visiting my office now?"

THERE WAS A SUBTLE CHANGE IN THE ATMOSPHERE WHEN SHE entered, an electric charge in the air, along with a lingering scent of licorice and vanilla that was more than a little appealing.

I'd met Angelique twice before when I was helping Frankie find her missing, dead sister.

This was an awesome woman, Poe's right hand it appeared, as fierce as he was. A no-nonsense lady with a keen sense of loyalty to her boss.

She was black, tall, stunning. She wore a black jacket over a simple white blouse above a long black silk skirt that flowed like slick oil down to her open-toed stiletto-heeled pumps. A silver necklace with a single black onyx stone lay at her collarbone, and she had a small tattoo there, a bird of prey, perhaps a hawk. She was a martial artist like Marsh and me, rumored to have exemplary skills. I'd gotten a glimpse of them when she'd caught me off balance on the roof of the Fairmount Hotel two years before.

She looked cold, aloof, an ice queen. But I felt she concealed a hidden warmth toward me, an unacknowledged attraction. There was a certain frisson I sensed on each of the two occasions we had shared the same space.

But she was a woman who played her cards close to the vest.

That was my explanation, anyway.

Poe gestured with his hand, offering her the seat opposite mine in front of his desk. She eased into the chair, lifted her skirt away, revealing lush, toned dark flesh beneath metallic gray stockings. She raised her long sinewy right leg and laid it over her just as muscly left.

I imagined she, too, could touch her palms to the floor, so there we were together, a flexible triumvirate.

"Angelique, could you fill Mr. Plank in on the situation? Please, leave nothing out."

She looked at him for a moment, their eyes danced, and at that moment, I wondered if they'd ever shared sheets. Poe's sexuality, like much else about him, was a mystery. He lived alone but was rumored to have lovers of both sexes.

Angelique turned her attention to me. Her almond-shaped eyes, there had to be an Asian influence along with the African American tint, took my measure. Her tongue slipped just over her lower lip, a tic, a gathering of her thoughts, and then she began.

Her voice was deep, with a faraway southern lilt to it, but refined, smoothed out, containing a dollop of honey and a bite of spice. South Texas all chummy with Jamaica. "Mr. Plank, it started—"

"Please, Angelique, Max."

"Mr. Plank," she said, not smiling. "I'd appreciate it if you listened silently until I finish."

I felt like I'd had the back of my hand spanked with a ruler. If I was going to get spanked, I didn't mind so much it being her. I glanced at Poe, who shot me a smile and shrugged his shoulders.

I pressed my forefinger and thumb together and drew a line in front of my lips, zipping.

She rolled her eyes at me.

"As I was saying, it started when Bobby came to see me about a month ago…"

She took almost ten minutes to lay it all out. I asked a couple of questions to be polite, then turned to Poe and told him there was nothing I could do for him.

"I'll double," he paused, scratched his cheek, "triple your usual fee. And if you find him within a week, there'll be a bonus," he said, playing with a folder on his desk, avoiding my eyes, like it was embarrassing to overpay for my services.

I didn't think there was anything to be ashamed about. In other circumstances, I would have caved into his request, despite my reservations about doing any more business with the man.

But there was Alexandra and Waimea Canyon.

"Generous of you, but I'm going away for a week. Anyway, why do you think I can find him when you and all your resources have had no luck?"

He teepeed his index fingers and brought them up to his lips, studying me for a few moments. "Don't be modest. I know how good you and your friend, Marsh, are at this kind of thing."

"Sorry. I'll be out of pocket."

He sighed. Poe is a man used to people doing his bidding.

He shook his head. "This is important. Very important. Tell me what I have to do to convince you."

"Nothing you can do."

"That's disappointing. Surprising also. I felt sure you would help me."

Angelique stayed motionless, her eyes fixed on a point somewhere behind Poe. Despite her lack of movement, there was a coiled spring tension vibe emanating from her body that made the hairs on my arms tingle.

"I've had this planned for a while. If you've had no luck in two weeks, call me again and maybe…"

"It can't wait. Thank you for your time. Angelique will see you out." He turned away and gave me the cold shoulder.

His voice was as icy as the inside of a meat locker. I'd seen it before. He could be the most polite, civilized human being on earth one moment, and then the next, turn into a stone-cold killer.

Talk about your moody gangsters.

Angelique rose, motioned with her hand, and followed me out of the office.

We shared a silent elevator ride, her licorice scent tickling my nose pleasantly, and she stayed with me until we reached the massive revolving glass doors leading out of Pirate's Cove.

I waved at her and said, "Bye," not expecting a reply.

She said, "If I were you, I'd reconsider."

I turned and looked back at her, but she'd already turned away. I watched her walk until she disappeared into the crowd near the blackjack tables. She moved gracefully, the motion of her voluptuous haunches a challenge and a dare echoing her words in my mind.

TWO

After leaving Pirate's Cove, I went home to *Acapella Blues*, a 42-foot houseboat, a re-imagined World War II lifeboat docked at the end of Pier 39 on San Francisco's Fisherman's Wharf where I faced a full day of long-deferred maintenance—washing, cleaning, painting, engine tuning, and general tinkering.

They say that when you own a house, upkeep is never-ending. That goes double if your house is situated on the water.

By the time the sun dipped toward the western horizon, my tasks were only half-done, but I was exhausted and ready for a nap in the hammock I sometimes unfurl on the bow. As I was about to do just that, my friend Marsh showed up with earth-shaking news.

We sat on the back deck of the boat with plates of garlic broccoli omelets I'd whipped up and watched the sunset and the surrounding panoply—sailors tying up their boats after a long day fishing, the myriad activities across the way from *Acapella* at Beer 39, specializing in craft brews and beer tchotchkes. On the wharf, people were milling about the Eagle Cafe, hankering after a seafood dinner and behind that, The Hard Rock Cafe drawing a crowd.

At the end of the pier, at the Sea Lion Center, said mammals lolled in the dying light, their sharp barks punctuating the sunset's bated breath air.

"You make a mean omelet, Plank," Marsh said, after making quick work of my cooking.

I raised my coffee mug to him.

Marsh was two years younger than me and looked five. He had dirty blond hair and golden, unblemished skin. His eyes were steely gray, appraising life and all those living it with a cool, hard matter-of-factness. His body wasn't overly muscled or bulky, but he was cut, lithe, and moved like a ballet dancer. He was a master of more esoteric martial arts than I had names for. He'd trained me, adding to my arsenal of basic but pretty effective moves.

"I'm getting married," he said, staring at his empty plate.

I dropped my mug, and it rolled across the deck, clattering to a stop at the bulwarks. My mouth was probably gaping wide open.

Marsh is the most confirmed bachelor I know. He'd been seeing a younger man, Tom, for the past couple of years, the longest relationship he's had since we met in our early twenties. He'd broken up with Tom several times, but they always got back on their emotional rollercoaster.

I didn't know the M word was in Marsh's vocabulary. It scared me a little because the M word is definitely not part of mine.

"What did you say?" I responded, dumbfounded.

He looked away, out toward Alcatraz Island, the prison turned hot tourist spot, about a mile away, with a frown on his face.

"Getting married," he responded, his eyes still lost at sea.

"Wow," I said.

He kept looking at Alcatraz.

"You seem overwhelmed with joy."

"Don't be an ass."

"You and Tom?"

He nodded.

"Great," I said, trying to give my voice a happy lilt. "Congratulations."

More stoic staring.

"Are you going to tell me?"

He took a deep breath through that noble Protestant nose of his and then let it out in a long sigh. "He asked me, and I said yes."

"How romantic."

"You're best man."

"I'm flattered."

"This is hard enough without you being a smart ass."

Wedding engagements are not normally made of such sweet sorrow.

"I'll take it seriously when you tell me why."

"Why," he said and looked me in the eye. "Tom wants to. He's asked me before. He doesn't give up. What the hell. I'm forty now. Maybe it's time. I like Tom."

"Well, if you like him, then you should marry him, no doubt. How many men have you really liked before?"

"Plank." He shook his head.

"Just trying to understand... You've always been even more down on the institution than me and that's saying something."

"I don't want to talk about it."

"When is it?"

"If Tom gets his way, before Christmas. He has a thing about Christmas. The way he tells it, his childhood, in New England, was out of a fairy tale."

"Well, they say opposites attract. Isn't the best man supposed to plan the bachelor party?"

"Grow up."

All children, except one, grow up, I thought.

I studied my friend for a moment and decided that something

was bothering him, and it went beyond this marriage thing. But I knew Marsh, and until he was ready to tell me, I wouldn't get any more information.

So I told him about my meeting with Poe.

"You said you wouldn't have anything to do with the man after all that stuff with Frankie," he said after I finished my summary.

"I'm not."

"Sounds like if you weren't going away, you would have taken it on."

"I don't know."

"Something about him fascinates you. Intrigues you." He paused, smiled. "Perhaps you just want to see more of Angelique."

I realized both those statements might hold a smidgen of truth, heretofore unacknowledged. Marsh sometimes seems to be able to access my unconscious thoughts and motivations. It's unnerving.

I shrugged. "Maybe I see it as part of keeping up with the crime scene in the city. He's often at least tangentially involved, even if his fingerprints are never present."

"I gather he was none too pleased with your soft refusal."

"Pissed him off." I told him about Angelique's parting advice that I reconsider. "Not that I'm worried about what he might do, but could you look into this Bobby thing a little? Find out what the word is around the casino. And anything you can find about the thefts. He says it was over a million bucks. Angelique described it as gambling related, so there were cheats at blackjack, roulette, and poker with some dealers involved. He said he hasn't reported it, which I don't believe. He probably did, but the police are keeping it under wraps for him. Anything you can find out about Bobby or the missing money might help me decide in case he asks again after I get back from Hawaii."

Marsh is wealthy and influential and connected as hell throughout the Bay Area and really, the country, if not the world.

He has a large staff of top professionals, either directly on the payroll or a phone call away, not only involved with his various real estate enterprises but also throughout the city's political and business and criminal trades.

He'd been special forces during part of the Afghanistan conflict and sometimes disappeared on what I assumed were covert missions initiated by some or other deep-cover government agency. He never talked about these activities. I don't think he wants me exposed to the risks.

He also has genius-level computer hackers at his command, including the fair and brilliant Portia, who had helped me on cases several times in the past few years.

He has access to manpower and resources that we mere mortals can only dream of.

"I'll see what I can see," he said.

Then he got up without another word and left.

I sat there for a long while thinking about Bobby and Poe and Angelique and Hawaii and Alexandra, not necessarily in that order.

But what really stuck in my craw was the fact that Marsh was somebody's fiancé.

It was mind-boggling.

THREE

I woke up with the soaring, squalling seagulls at half-past six, put on shorts and a black t-shirt—Springsteen and his guitar jumping in rock 'n roll joy, and trudged out to the back deck barefoot.

I ran through my regularly prescribed forty-five minutes of yoga, alternating power yoga vinyasa moves with asanas heavy on joint stretching. Afterward, I sat in a double-seated pigeon pose for ten minutes, breathing in and out through my nose, pushing worldly thoughts away from my mind.

Didn't work all that well. Sometimes it does.

As I was trying to attain a semblance of nirvanic calm, a woman's voice interrupted. She was standing on the pier, watching me.

"Max Plank?" she said, in a high, wistful voice that matched her cherubic face.

I sat there all pigeon-posed and nodded.

"My name is Paula Fenderdale. Do you have a few minutes?"

The name rang a bell, and I struggled unsuccessfully to place the note. I nodded and waved her onboard, anyway.

WE SAT INSIDE IN MY RUSTIC LITTLE CABIN. I'D REDESIGNED THE place over the past few months, or, rather, Alexandra and Frankie, with an assist from Meiying, my friend and neighbor living on a nearby boat, had all ganged up on me and forced some changes.

I didn't mind. Interior decor is not exactly in my bailiwick.

And they hadn't overdone the girly stuff. There were now more pictures on the gnarly wood walls—mainly photos from Alexandrea's overseas assignments—giraffes and elephants in African grasslands, single-humped camels in Arabian deserts, pandas in Washington zoos, and pelicans with beaks full of fish right here in San Francisco Bay, along with some of Frankie's school etchings and shots of scenic Fisherman's Wharf. There was more seating: two new barstools, a cushy chair beside my old battered couch, re-covered in brown leather. An antique desk had been refinished and stained a dark walnut color and sat in a corner beneath the skylight. Everything else was rearranged, and just a tad tidier and cleaner.

It still seemed like a cozy place to hang your hat, keeping most of the down-home humbleness I liked.

I turned my attention to Ms. Fenderdale. From up close she still evidenced a skosh of the angelic, her auburn hair tied back flat against her skull and secured with a brass clasp. She had round cheeks and plump lips and a distinctive pug nose that seemed off center. Her eyes were large and shaded light blue. Her dress, a solid blue sheath, covered her from collarbone to ankles. The only decorations were a silver bracelet and a matching necklace. She wore no wedding ring.

She exuded a quiet but pronounced sensuality, something in the way she moved, in her eyes, that seemed barely contained.

I pointed at the cushy chair, and after she'd settled in, I plopped myself on one of the bar stools.

"Anything I can get for you before—"

"No, thank you, Mr. Plank. I want to get right to the point and then get out of your hair."

That suited me, so I nodded and waited for her to embellish.

"You know my father, Bobby Fenderdale."

The bell note chimed clear to me now. This was Poe's niece, his brother's daughter. Poe's real name, which he'd shed many years ago during his westward voyage, was Lawrence Fenderdale.

"I didn't know Bobby had a daughter your age."

"My mom was his first wife. They were both nineteen. It only lasted long enough to have me. My mom raised me, but Dad stayed in touch."

Bobby'd found two women to marry him. *Stranger things.*

"Did Poe send you?"

"No."

"How did you find me then?"

"My uncle mentioned you, but he didn't send me here. He told me he'd asked you to help find my father, but that you'd refused."

"That's correct. I'm afraid I'll be out of town for a while, so it would be impossible for me to—"

"My father is in real trouble. If someone doesn't find him soon. Within the next few days..." Her eyes welled up with tears, a single drop escaping, running down her cheek. She closed her eyes, clasped her hands in her lap, and breathed a calming breath out through her nose. "My uncle told me you are the best private detective in the city."

As she gave me the full sympathy of her azure orbs, I wondered if Poe had really told her that, and if he did, whether he believed it.

I believed it, so wasn't shocked when others recognized my skills.

In my trade, false modesty used to curry faint praise has no currency. That's true of most lines of work, but when it comes to criminal or murderous shenanigans and their denouement, why bother?

"I don't have much money, and I'm sure my uncle offered you more than I ever could."

I slipped off the stool, went to my desk, and fingered through a Rolodex. I paused twice and wrote two names and phone numbers on a piece of notepaper. I returned to stand in front of Paula Fenderdale. "This isn't about money. I'm just not going to be here for more than a week and so there's no way I can help. There are other good detectives in the city. Here are a couple of names. They'll do a good job for you."

They weren't Max Plank, but they were trustworthy, reliable, and diligent.

If you need a decent vacuum cleaner for a fair price, these two would do a reasonable job of sucking up your filth.

She didn't look at me and didn't reach for the paper in my hand. Instead, she wiped her eyes clear of tears, opened a small pocketbook, and removed a thin cellophane packet of pink Kleenex. She blew her nose, wadded up the tissue, and folded it back into the pouch.

"I didn't really want to get into this, but I guess there's no way around it."

I stifled an exasperated sigh in mid-breath. I didn't want to hear what she had to say. "Ms. Fenderdale... Paula, I'm sympathetic, but there's really nothing—"

"Please!"

Startled, I frowned at her. She didn't exactly scream her plea, but it was only a note on the scale away from hysteria.

With trembling lips and hurried words, she said, "Please, please, just listen for a minute." Her face was a mask of such anguish that only a heartless bastard could refuse her.

I considered it but turned and sat back down on the bar stool and nodded for her to continue.

"Thank you," she murmured, gathered herself again with a deep inhalation. "My dad showed up unexpectedly at my apartment about a week from last Thursday. He's never done that before. I hadn't seen him in a couple of months."

"How often do you normally see him?"

Why was I asking questions?

"Usually at least once or twice a month. We're pretty close. We text every couple of days, just check-ins, and he calls me at least once a week."

"Go on," I said.

"He looked terrible. He seemed to have aged ten years in two months. I'd never seen him look so bad, even when he..." She looked away, out the porthole, biting her lip.

"Poe told me about his problems in the past with cocaine, said that he'd struggled for a while but was in recovery." I followed her gaze out the porthole to the calm sea and beyond, images of Hawaii and Alexandra and me in idyllic and suggestive embraces fought for primacy over this poor young woman's worry about her daddy.

"Yeah, he was. It had been more than a year since he'd had any. He smoked pot, but that was all. He'd been trying so hard, and it wasn't easy. He didn't want to disappoint his brother, who'd given him such a big chance to start over."

I glanced back at her. She was looking at me with such earnestness, such yearning, that I had to look away. I have a soft spot for kitties and puppies and stray women, sure. I admit it. I don't like kids or women being abused. Sue me. But nobody was being violated here. It was just another case of a man failing, not strong enough to overcome his weaknesses.

I'm not a therapist. My boat isn't the site of a twelve-step program.

"So he was back on it?" I asked after she remained stuck in her head for longer than I was comfortable with.

"He said no. But I could tell, all the signs were there. He was hyper, he couldn't sit still. His pupils were dilated." Paula shook her head. "I don't know if he'd just started up or if he'd been slipping up for a while. I'd guess it was very recent because my uncle would have noticed. He'd warned him, told him what he wouldn't tolerate. When I met with him, my uncle said nothing about that, so I guess he didn't know."

Poe hadn't mentioned that his brother had fallen off the wagon either. Still, this wasn't a shock or a reason for me to step in.

"I'm sorry that your dad is still struggling, but—"

"That's not the most important thing," she hurried to say. "But it makes what he told me even more urgent. More dangerous."

Despite myself, I said, "Tell me."

"He said he'd gotten involved with some bad people. He said it was a long story, some guys he knew from years back when he was struggling with his 'habit,' as he referred to it. He said that these people had done him a favor and now, recently, had asked for a favor in return."

"Did he say who these men were?"

"He wouldn't tell me. Said the less I knew the better. He told me he didn't have much of a choice. And he didn't think it was a big deal, really. It had something to do with the casino. Dad said it was just in the past few days when he realized how they'd used him, how his favor had hurt the casino. He was afraid. Afraid of them and afraid of what his brother would do if he found out that Dad was involved."

"It has to be the thefts, the game cheats that Poe told me about. Did he tell you anything about what he did, what the favor was?"

"No. Just that someone had fooled him. He couldn't believe how stupid he'd been. He was desperate, Mr. Plank. I think it made him go back on the coke because he thought there was no way out."

Nothing forced him to shoot up, but I didn't bother pointing that out to her.

"I told him to go to his brother and tell him everything. To explain what happened. I told him that my uncle would forgive him if he told the truth and explained how he hadn't known, how he'd been fooled. My uncle isn't a bad guy, and I know he loves Dad."

She was partially right. Poe is a sociopath, albeit a very ambiguous and complex one, but it seemed he loved or at least had feelings for his brother. But as far as forgiveness goes, I had my doubts. In the long run, if he felt betrayed, whether intentionally or not, blood ties wouldn't matter a whit to him.

"I gather he didn't take your advice."

She shook her head, nibbling on her thumbnail with her front teeth. "He said he'd think about it. I tried to get him to stay with me for the night, but he said he would try to see if he could fix things. He said he had an appointment with one of the guys, one who wasn't so bad, and he had an idea, something that might just make things better and, if it worked out, then he'd talk to his brother. I was afraid for him because he was so agitated. But I couldn't stop him, and he left, and I haven't seen or heard from him since."

"And that was...?"

"A week ago Thursday, so about six days now."

That was too long. Much too long.

"Did he say anything more about the appointment or this man he was meeting?"

"No. I asked him, but he wouldn't tell me."

"So your dad had a meeting with some guy, a man who'd gotten him involved with cheating the casino, and he hasn't been seen since." I let that and its implications sit there in the air between us.

"He's not dead if that's what you think. I'd know it if he was."

I've had many people tell me the same thing about loved ones. Some of them have been right. Others, not so much.

"Did you tell Poe all this?"

She looked away again and placed both hands on top of her head, maybe trying to keep something in her brain from bubbling over and out. Finally, she said, "No, I didn't. I was…afraid to."

Good thinking.

"I didn't know enough about what was going on. I wanted to tell him. I may still if you turn me down. Maybe it will help him find Dad. No matter what it is, I'm sure that the two of them can work it out together."

I'd heard nothing that would make me cancel my trip to Hawaii. I felt sympathy for her and Bobby, he'd gotten in way over his head, but there wasn't any reason for me to get involved.

I suddenly noticed the piece of paper in my hand with the second and third best detectives in San Francisco written on it. I held it up to her and said, "These men can help you, Paula. I'm sure they'd do as well as I."

Little white lies are often just the right elixir to ease the jammed joints that can gum up human relations.

Again, she gave me those soft, yearning puppy dog eyes, followed by a voice not much more than a murmur. "Mr. Plank, I'm begging you. Can you just spend a little time before you leave even? I have a hunch where you might start. I told my uncle, and he told me his men checked it out but got nowhere. I've been there myself twice this week. But I don't know what I'm doing. Being a woman in this place doesn't help. Can you at least take an hour out of your day, today? I know it's asking a lot. But just go to this one place where someone might know more about Dad and what happened. I'm sure. You're the best, right? If anyone can get the truth out of this place, it's you. Please."

It was less than twenty-four hours until I was scheduled to pick up Alexandra for our afternoon flight to Honolulu. No time to start an investigation of any sort. Time only to attend to some last-minute trip details, pack, and get ready to leave. It would be a total waste of time to go to wherever this place was and ask questions when Poe's men, motivated and thorough, and Paula herself, had already tried.

Did she think I could pull a rabbit out of a hat in the blink of an eye? Did I look like a magician?

That's not how an investigation works. A case usually relies on the slow, methodical gathering of information through interviews with people, likely and unlikely, and the resulting details sometimes yield clues, but clues were subtle things, details that most people didn't notice or made no sense unless you thought outside the box, knew that there was no box.

Finding a missing person or solving a murder took time and patience and keen attention to people, places, and things, most of which needed to be sifted through and then discarded, proven worthless. Some of which held the promise of the one detail or clue that lit a fire under other clues and, with a little luck and persistence, allowed the detective to have that ah-hah moment that one lives for.

There was no magic involved.

Not usually.

I won't say never because that's the thing with magic—once in a while it'll rear up and kiss you on the ass.

I told Paula Fenderdale that she'd bought a couple of hours of my time and promised that I'd call her before I left town.

FOUR

efore I left *Acapella Blues*, I called Marsh to tell him about
my meeting with Paula Fenderdale and my plans to
investigate just a little, but he couldn't talk. He told me to
drop by Kabuki, the nightclub and, naturally, Kabuki theater that
he was developing with our good friend, Dao.

When I got there, both of them were up on the stage, with the
magnificent, shimmery bronze-toned theater curtain wavering
over their heads like a sail.

They'd been working on it for more than a year, struggling
through San Francisco's labyrinthine inspection and permitting
process while trying to satisfy Marsh's commitment to perfection
and Dao's sense of authentic Kabuki style.

I joined them on stage, and Dao turned to me immediately and
said, "You heard the happy, amazing news?"

I gave him a blank look.

He grasped Marsh's elbow. "Our friend is getting married."

Marsh looked away, his eyes searching for a distraction, a way
to deflect Dao's excitement. He spotted a man with a utility belt
and a hard hat struggling with some cable wires in a dimly lit

corner behind the shimmery curtain and shouted, "Tony, you need help?"

"No, boss, I got it. Though it would be nice if Josie could get us more twelve-gauge ethereal."

"How much?"

"Double the last order."

"You got it."

Dao shook Marsh's elbow lightly. "Such a pleasant surprise. Tommy is such a nice boy. Meiying loves him."

Marsh was paying no mind, his glance bouncing around the building, looking for a diversion.

A proud groom he did not seem to be.

Just then Meiying, Dao's wife, appeared to make things even more awkward.

She lit up the room. Even in her late sixties, she's still a beauty, a lovely little Asian spark plug. But she carries her Beijing culture and manners with her. She was sent over in her twenties to marry Dao, an arranged marriage that turned out to be love at first sight for Dao.

She marched right up to her husband and reached for his hand. He took it, his eyes glowing with the pride and the satisfaction always evident when he was with her.

She turned her gaze to me and said, "See? You have no excuse now, Plank. Shame on you."

For a moment, I felt confused but then she added, "Marsh has shown you up. He is a man. You are still a boy."

Meiying has been trying to marry me off almost since the day I met her and Dao a few years ago. They have their boat, *Sweet and Sour*, docked not too far from mine on Fisherman's Wharf, although their floating home is decidedly more luxurious than my modest digs. Dao was wealthy before his fortieth birthday and still makes beaucoup bucks as a freelance investment advisor to people even richer than he is.

I love Meiying, but she drives me crazy. She seldom lets up and has tried to set me up with women of just about every nationality and culture. They're always young, gorgeous, and smart. What more could a man want?

Since I'm relatively committed to Alexandra, and now our adopted daughter, Frankie, she's let up on the blind date arranging, but she thinks the fact that I haven't asked Alexandra to marry me borders on the criminal.

In her world, a man like me deserves to be locked up, less I infect other eligible bachelors with my amoral lifestyle.

I looked at Dao, who gave me a sympathetic shrug of his shoulders.

Marsh, who was almost impossible to fluster, looked like he wanted to crawl under the stage.

I understood Meiying. She was from another place and time, but I didn't understand Marsh's uncharacteristic, rash action, which, by his demeanor, he knew to be batshit crazy.

Meiying took Marsh in a hug. He stood there, his arms at his side, her head reaching the top of his ribcage, as she murmured, "We are so happy for you Marsh. *Sweet and Sour* is yours for the wedding."

I guess her views weren't wholly traditional, as you'd expect she'd have a problem with gay marriage, but she loves the Marsh man so much, and not only because he'd twice saved their lives. She was overjoyed that he would be happy. And she equated adult human happiness with marriage.

It had worked for her, after all.

She looked up at him, and he looked into her eyes, although he still looked like he'd rather be anywhere but here.

She said, "When?"

Marsh shrugged.

"You have it on *Sweet and Sour?*"

"I'll ask Tommy."

"Good. You get married soon, no?"

"Tommy wants to get married just before Christmas."

"Wonderful. I help you plan."

"Tommy's taking care of all that."

His voice was flat, bordering on strangled.

Meiying didn't seem to pick up on the negative vibes. She knew Marsh was unusual. And her confidence that marriage was the cure for any man's problems let her thoughts sail above any present-day storm.

She let him go turned to me with a disapproving look. "What you think Alexandra think?"

I didn't think. I hadn't thought. She'd think it was as inexplicable as I did.

But Meiying might have a point. I knew without her saying it that Alexandra wanted a permanent commitment from me.

At least until recently, I'd been sure she'd swoon if I got down on one knee with a little box in my hand.

But, as I've said, the mood around the house had altered subtly. That was my fault, and Hawaii would fix it.

Meiying added, "I tell you what she think—"

"Meiying," Dao whispered, "let's celebrate Marsh and Tommy. Max can wait."

Meiying frowned, looked at Dao, pursed her lips disapprovingly. But she nodded. "Okay. We celebrate Marsh today. We knock sense into Plank tomorrow."

Dao said, "Let's go to the Rusty Root and have lunch. Have you told Bo?"

Marsh replied, "No."

Not a big surprise.

Meiying clapped her hands, signaling that nothing could be more fun than spreading the good news to another friend.

Bo was one of my best friends, a musician in a semi-successful band he and I had both been in in our twenties. He now owned a great restaurant on Fisherman's Wharf and played in another band on the side.

The Rusty Root was also where Dao and I convened for our ongoing Cribbage mano-a-mano every Wednesday at noon.

Although the combat between us was usually not much of a fight. Dao won upward of eighty percent of the games, and over the past year I hadn't been able to up my winning percentage more than a few measly points.

I told Dao and Meiying and three members of the Kabuki team, the primary choreographer, the producer, and director, to go on ahead to the Rusty Root, and that Marsh and I would join them.

After they'd left, the two of us sat on the stage while I filled him in on Paula Fenderdale's visit.

"Do you ever turn down a woman in need?" Marsh asked, but I knew it was rhetorical, so I didn't answer.

"Any other reason you changed your mind?" he added, then shouted, "Hey, Tony, those two by fours you were waiting for are supposed to be delivered today so we can start on the balance beam architecture."

"Great, boss," Tony shouted back while traversing the back of the stage with a long metal beam wavering over his shoulder.

I waited until Tony disappeared backstage and said, "I don't know. She seemed sincere. She just wanted me to check out one place, spend a couple of hours asking questions, see what I could see. She's really worried about her dad, and it sounds like she has cause."

"Yeah. Cause. Is this because of Poe? Like you're trying to help him without directly helping him?"

"No. I know Bobby too. He's a mess, but likable. Being Poe's brother can't be easy on a guy like that. I have a little time before we leave, so why not see if I can help his daughter and him?"

"Why not," Marsh repeated. "Que Sera."

"Will I be pretty?"

Marsh laughed. "That's it, isn't it? You want to please. You want everyone to think you're pretty."

"You know better than that."

Above the smell of spanking-fresh wood and swirling sawdust that permeated the theater under construction, the scent of pizza tickled my nose. The guys in the back had probably ordered out, and I realized how hungry I was.

"So, can you check out Paula Fenderdale? Here's her phone number. She seemed sincere, and I'm sure there's no problem, but run her anyway." I got up, stretched my hands over my head while rolling up onto my tippy toes, flexing up and down. "Let's go see Bo. I need some linguini and mussels and we can tell him your good news."

"Yes, to the mussels. I'm not going to tell him a damn thing."

"You don't have to worry about that. By the time we get there, Meiying will have him planning your bachelor party at the Rusty Root."

Marsh shook his head dismissively and took off.

I followed in his footsteps, wondering at the profound strangeness of life itself.

FIVE

fter lunch, where Bo Fiddler had provided tasty platters of mussels and linguine and calamari to all of us, and been as gobsmacked as me about Marsh's coming nuptials, while Marsh sat stoically under the weight of a lot of unwanted attention, I took my Ducati motorcycle down the 101 to San Francisco's peninsula, in San Bruno, near SFO Airport.

I sat in my car parked at a meter across the street from the place that Paula Fenderdale had sent me—Matthew's Manufacturing Muscles gymnasium.

Three points for alliteration.

I'd normally have asked a client in her circumstances for a key or other means of access to her dad's apartment. I didn't even know what town he lived in.

If someone disappears, the best place to start your search is the place he last called home. Often, but not always, there are hints— subtle, hidden, or right out in the open, clues how to proceed. Answers to questions you might not have even thought to ask. Perhaps they might not reveal where to start looking, but the mysteries of a troubled inner life or the whys and hows, the motivations behind the disappearance, if you know where to look and how to pay attention, might just be lying there in plain sight.

But I didn't want to visit Bobby's house. I knew that if I picked up the scent of the mystery there, I'd have a hard time letting go.

THE GYM WAS BOOKMARKED BETWEEN A NINJA SHUSHI AND TOFU bar and a Japanese restaurant, which seemed redundant. Directly across the street was a small family-owned casino, Flapjack Fred's, which had been around for more than a hundred years. It had started out as a pool hall and betting parlor where it was rumored the patriarch of the family used to say if he lost a big bet, he'd pay off in pancakes.

Now it was a full-fledged, but relatively tiny, casino.

My eyes roved between the scruffy gym and the pedestrian off-white brick casino exterior, which looked more like the entrance to a bar, and I felt a sense of dread bubbling up inside me.

Clues. Damn clues.

It seemed too much of a coincidence that this was where Bobby's daughter thought her dad might hang out, or at least be familiar with. A casino totally unlike Poe's glamorous tricked-out high-end place, but still, a brother-in-arms.

What were the chances that there was no connection between the two gambling joints? I pictured Poe wincing at that term for describing his pride and joy.

A man lay sprawled on his side on the ground beside the entrance to Matthew's Manufacturing Muscles. His shock of grayish-black hair looked as if somebody had plugged his head into a wall socket. A large nasty purple bruise swelled on his right temple. Dried blood stained the cavity of his visible ear. His head and legs peeked out from beneath a large plastic bag from which spilled a Styrofoam egg container, a box of candy Easter eggs, a half-empty bottle of no-name whiskey, an open box of Cheerios, a flyer advertising a $2.99 breakfast at Fred's Flapjacks, and a crushed can of Mountain Dew. A mangy white cat lay curled into the crook of his arm.

Despite his location, it didn't look like he'd worked out in a very long time.

I dropped to my haunches, dug his arm out from beneath the plastic bag, and found his wrist. He had a pulse, but it was fast and uneven.

"Sir?" I said, leaning toward his face. The strong smell of urine mixed with unbathed male made me hold my breath. I shook his shoulder. He let out a loud snort, mumbled what sounded like, "Shitmeister," but kept his eyes closed. He rolled to the left until his face was pressed against the cat's ass. It didn't seem to bother the feline.

I rose and entered the gym through the smoky glass door plastered with faded photos of overly muscled men flexing. There was the requisite photo of our former governor, Arnold, among them. I was sure he'd never set foot inside, but he'd presumably started out at a place in Austria very much like this.

Inside, I was confronted with a facility that held no truck with fitness trends. It was small and compact, fifteen hundred square feet devoted to one particular thing.

And that thing, unsurprisingly, was building muscle. You weren't going to find a lot of women hanging out here.

The place reeked of sweat and testosterone and antiseptic cleaner.

There wasn't a Stairmaster or an elliptical or a rowing machine in sight. Not even a treadmill.

What there was was a lot of dumbbells.

And I'm not just talking about the clientele.

There were bench presses and barbells and kettlebells and pull up bars and squat racks. There were tires wrenched from the chassis of eighteen wheelers.

And weights. Lots and lots of weights.

Nothing fancy or new about them. They were old and worn and mostly made of cast iron.

No frills, but they'd fulfill Matthew's promise to manufacture muscles if used consistently and properly.

It was dusky in there, dust motes filling the air beneath overhead bulky canisters made of plastic and metal housing harsh oversized lights illuminating the equipment like an off-off-off-Broadway stage. The floor was a faded, stained black-and-white linoleum, with chunks of it worn away or ripped asunder.

A half-dozen men were working out, either slinging free weights or grunting and straining on bench presses.

I spotted a white door in the back fronting a small office with a glass wall. I threaded my way through the equipment, which seemed to be arranged as a kind of parcourse, a test of agility. The stench of body odor was as strong as the stink of urine coming from the homeless man outside.

The door was unmarked and half-open, and I gave it a nudge and stepped through into a roughly eight by ten space crammed with bookshelves holding office supplies and a few faded paperback body building books. A bunch of metal filing cabinets filled up wall space, along with dust mops, an ancient Hoover vacuum cleaner, and a small metal desk shoved beside the door.

The desk was immaculately clean. It sported all the usual accouterments like pens and staplers and paper clips, along with a photo of a lovely young auburn-haired woman holding a Havanese puppy in front of what looked like Lake Tahoe. A Mac laptop centered the desk.

Sitting at it was a man probably in his mid-fifties, bald, and shredded like a chunk of granite meticulously molded by Michelangelo.

I can play the alliteration game too.

The man looked up from his laptop and frowned. He had a nose that had been broken in several places and a prominent brow, along with thin lips and a strong chin. His eyes were dark. They'd seen it all and remained unimpressed.

"Matthew?" I tried.

"He's dead," the man replied in a shockingly high-pitched voice that probably was the reason he started weightlifting. All that being made fun of in middle school for having a girly voice.

No one was going to mess with him now.

He just stared at me with an annoyed expression on his face, not bothering to introduce himself or welcome me to his little gym.

"My name is Max Plank."

That didn't alter his expression.

"Are you the owner?"

He waited a long time but eventually said, "Yeah. I guess so."

I was surprised there wasn't a line of hopeful lifters threading all the way out the door and spilling into the street, clamoring to get into this customer-friendly place.

"There's a homeless man outside, lying in front of your front door. Looks like he's hurt."

"Yeah?" he said.

"Yeah," I said back. "Didn't you have to step over him to get in here this morning?"

He raised his eyebrows, and his rock-like facial structure tightened. He put a foot out and rolled his chair away from the desk and toward me. He crossed his arms across his chest, displaying pectorals bursting beneath his tight black Matthew's Manufacturing Muscles t-shirt. His biceps bulged like balloons.

It was an impressive display, and I reacted accordingly.

"So they called you a sissy a lot when you were in school."

That expanded his range of retorts. "What the fuckin' hell?"

His face flushed crimson, and his massive hands clutched the chair's armrests. He leapt to his feet and stood trembling in front of me.

He hadn't made peace with his past. I doubt he'd even seen a therapist.

I like to make a strong first impression on people, but, as Marsh tells me, sometimes I get a little carried away.

"Lookit, I meant no insult. What you've done with yourself in the face of all that bullying is admirable. And there's nothing wrong with being a sissy anyway, is there, really?"

I thought he was going to lunge at me with a fist, and I shifted my right foot subtly forward, preparing myself.

But he surprised me. He released his clenched fists, snorted through his nose, and chuckled. He was consciously calming himself.

Maybe he had seen a therapist or was a practitioner of meditation.

All that remarkable musculature seemed to relax, and he eased back down into the chair. He sat there for a few seconds, gathering himself, and then looked at me with a half-smile and muttered, "What the fuck you want?"

"Thinking about joining your gym. Friend of mine recommended it."

"Fuck," he said.

Nothing wrong with the words "fuck" or "yeah," but this guy was taking the fine art of conversation to a whole new level of brute conciseness.

"Yeah. Bobby Fenderdale. He comes here and told me I should check it out. So here I am. I like what you've done with the place." I turned and looked back out at the gym. "Simple, old-fashioned, but to-the-point."

"We're full," he mumbled.

I turned and looked at him, then turned back and looked out

through the glass, then looked back at him, then back out, then back at him, then back out.

He caught my drift. "Funny guy. Just cuz there ain't a lot of guys here now doesn't mean we aren't full. We're full. Damn full. Give me your name and I'll put you on our list. Anybody quits, I call you when your turn comes."

"That sounds amazing," I said. This hadn't gone as I expected. I'd chosen the wrong tack. "All right. Let me be honest with you. You know Bobby, right?"

He was shuffling around in his desk, probably looking for a waiting list I was sure didn't exist. He didn't answer me.

"Bobby's disappeared and I'm looking for him. Could you tell me the last time he was here? The last time you saw him?"

He stopped rifling through papers and looked up at me. "I don't know."

"Look, I apologize. Sometimes I put my foot in my mouth. It's a bad habit."

He looked up at me reflectively and said, "Foot in mouth disease."

Wow. I'd completely misjudged him. He had wit, if not charm. "May I ask your name?"

He stifled a little sigh and murmured, "Leslie. Leslie Meadows."

I almost lost it, but with a great force of will, restrained myself. It must have been hell for him. Sounding like Truman Capote and saddled with a girl's name. The brutally long hours he'd spent sculpting his body must have seemed an appropriate response, an overcompensation that fixed what you could see but probably made what you couldn't worse.

I have a bachelor's degree in Psychology, obviously.

"Leslie, really, Bobby's daughter and brother and friends are really worried about him and would really appreciate any information you could provide."

"Bobby has a daughter?" he said.

I nodded. I remembered her telling me she'd visited this place a couple of times recently to talk to people here about her father. Why hadn't she chatted up the inimitable Leslie?

"Yes. Do you remember the last time you saw him?"

"Couple weeks ago."

"How often did he come in?"

"Two, three times a week."

"For how long has he been coming here?"

"Few months."

"Do you have any idea where he might be now?"

He shook his head.

"Do you know any places he used to hang out? Anything he mentioned, things he liked to do?"

Leslie lowered his chin. "We weren't best buddies or anything. I showed him how to lift. We shot the breeze a few times. I don't know much about him other than that."

"Anything you can remember about how he acted or what he said the last time he was here?"

He screwed up his face, racking his brain for memories. "Naw. Nothing."

"Was he friends with any of your other clients?" I turned and pointed to the lifters outside. "Any of those guys?"

"Probably. He was a talker. Talked too much as far as I was concerned. I'd ask Carlos out there, the Latin dude with the slicked-back hair. He's a big talker too, and the two of them sometimes did more chatting than lifting."

"Thanks," I said as sincerely as I could manage. "Can I give you my number?" I didn't wait for a response, just dropped my card on his desk. A simple blue card suggestive of the sea with my name and cell phone number. "If you remember anything at all about Bobby, call me. His family would really be grateful."

He picked up a pair of reading glasses and squinted at the card. "You a friend of his or some kind of detective or something?"

"A little of both," I said.

I turned away, and as I passed out of the threshold to his office, he called out, "Hey, he used to go across the street to eat now and then. Don't know if he played the tables there or not. But he liked their breakfast special."

"Great. Thanks. You've helped."

"Yeah. The breakfast special's good. Two eggs any style, bacon, hash browns, toast, juice, all for $2.99."

Suddenly Leslie had turned chummy for no reason I could fathom. I had a tendency to grow on people, but this seemed odd.

"I'll give it a try. Thanks," I said.

As I reached out to grab the door, Leslie added, "I called the cops to come and help out with Robert out front. He's a regular here, but he must have gotten into trouble last night. They're slow to react these days when it comes to the homeless."

I turned back and smiled at him. "Good man," I said and went out to talk to Carlos, the Latin dude.

SIX

Carlos was eager to help, but had little to add to Leslie's information.

He confirmed that he and Bobby had been gym buddies, but he knew little about his life outside the gym. They talked mostly about politics, the 49ers, women, and lifting.

They agreed that politics was crazier than anything, except for women, and that lifting was life-changing, and the 49ers were shit.

Carlos liked Bobby but thought he had some troubles. He couldn't elaborate, just mentioned he was anxious, especially recently. They rarely saw each other outside of the gym, only a few meals together across the street at the casino.

He also knew nothing about Bobby having a grown daughter.

I wondered if Paula had been telling me the truth about coming here to find her father. I didn't know why she'd lie, but I didn't like it. I was glad that Marsh would check her out.

On my way out, I called the San Bruno police department to report the sad condition of Robert the homeless. I figured a follow-up call to Leslie's might light a fire under them. I checked on Robert once more, stuffed a ten-dollar bill in his coat pocket, and then wandered across the street to check out the breakfast special at Fred's Flapjack Casino.

I promised myself that this would be it. My search for Bobby would end right here at Fred's. Anything I turned up, I'd hand back over to his daughter and whatever investigator she hired. I needed to get home and get ready for Hawaii. I needed to call Alexandra and...well, tell her...

But that could probably wait until we were in Aloha land.

It turned out I was ten minutes past the twelve-noon cutoff time for the special. I could still get eggs and all sorts of pancakes, but the price was no longer special.

I ate some oatmeal pancakes and had a big cup of burnt coffee in a well-used white mug while taking stock of my surroundings. Just like Matthew's gym, Fred's was a throwback.

It was more a card club than a full-fledged casino. There were poker and blackjack and Baccarat tables. The place was dimly lit, gaudily carpeted, and, at least, at the moment, a sparsely populated gambling den.

There were about twenty tables altogether with dealers at only three of them and only a dozen patrons present. There were two restaurants, the coffee shop I was in, and an Italian spot, Frederico's Villa, on the other side of the casino.

In the middle of the main floor beneath a large neo-Baroque candelabra was a glass-enclosed booth with flashing neon lights proclaiming *Jackpots!* A bored-looking young blond-haired woman in a black evening dress leaned against the side of the booth studying her iPhone.

A grand piano sat beneath a gauzy spotlight near the western wall. A nook beside it featured a bar covered in black vinyl with large metallic nails holding it down. A backdrop of mirrored shelves stowing liquor bottles glistened in the half-light. A tall, slim attractive older woman, also wearing a black dress with a pronounced V-cut, polished beer mugs at the bar while a distinguished looking black man in a tuxedo sat at the piano playing notes softly and singing to himself.

I finished my flapjacks, paid my bill, and wandered over to the bar.

The bartender tendered a sweet smile and a welcoming hello. There were wrinkles at the corners of her eyes and lips. She was probably in her mid-forties and looking good. The low-cut dress allowed a view of the top of a small but nicely shaped bosom.

"Selma," I said, reading the name tag pinned right beside her cleavage. "Can I bother you for a cranberry juice?"

"My pleasure," she said, in a rich, husky voice. She fixed it up for me all fancy with a twist of lime and a little rainbow-colored umbrella floating amidst the ice cubes. Looking at her creation, I felt kinda special.

When she handed it to me, I thanked her and introduced myself with a proffered hand. "I'm Max."

She looked at it for a moment, then touched her fingers lightly to mine.

"How long have you been working here, Selma?"

Her eyes sparkled, or maybe it was just the light. "Almost five years."

"Like it?"

"Mostly. Meet some interesting characters."

"You like that? Meeting characters."

"Sure. Beats working in an office."

"I hear you. Selma, could I ask you a question?"

"Ask away." She picked up another beer mug, held it up the light, and polished it.

"I was wondering if you remember one particular guy who's been coming in here now and then, name of Bobby Fenderdale?"

She stopped rubbing, scrutinized my face for a moment, trying to figure out who I was. She didn't ask the question I expected though. "What's he look like?"

I described him in brief, and Selma said there were more than a few who resembled that description, but she couldn't say she knew much about any of them.

"There's a steady stream of men who come here, especially at night."

"Bobby was here mostly in the mornings. He liked the breakfast special."

A man stepped out from a darkened hallway behind the bar. It was dark back there in the nook, and I hadn't noticed the passageway. He was young, in his twenties, and had long sideburns and a handlebar mustache. He wore a cheap suit and a skinny red tie over a blue denim shirt. He looked at me for a moment longer than he should have and then barked at Selma, "Did you finish everything up for the party tonight?"

"Mostly. I still have to check on the printed menus and make sure the extra liquor is delivered and go pick up the favors and then do the flapjack thing on the napkins," Selma said.

"Don't you think you should get moving then?"

"It's under control, Randy."

"Better be," he growled, smirked at me, and disappeared back in the hole he'd crawled out of.

Selma sighed.

"That the boss?"

"His son. The boss has got class that wasn't passed down to Randy."

"Who's the boss?"

"Fred, Jr."

"Fred Flapjack, Jr."

She laughed. "Yeah. That's him. Only he goes by the last name Coleman."

"Do you think the piano player might know the guy I'm looking for?"

She looked over at the man seated at the piano, who was gently stroking the keys and singing "Stormy Weather" in a soft voice. She shrugged.

"What's his name?"

"That's Maximum Joe. He's been playing piano here and all over the Bay Area for the past hundred years."

"Nice talking with you. And thanks for the cranberry juice." I offered my hand again, and this time she gave me her whole palm and the benefit of her thumb running along the side of my baby finger.

"Aren't you going to ask me out?" she said, her voice even huskier than before.

I felt my cheeks redden, and I left my hand in hers for a few seconds as her nice thumb continued to play footsie with my finger. "Sorry. I'm going to be getting on a plane to go with my girlfriend to Hawaii tomorrow.

"Tomorrow is tomorrow. Now is now," she said, her thumb no longer rubbing, but lifted just above my hand, a promise if I responded properly to her common sense observation about the nature of time.

"I don't think my girlfriend would see it that way."

She pursed her lips into a pout. Slipped her hand out from beneath mine. I felt a little pang of loss. "Just my luck," she said.

"Selma, you dodged a bullet. Don't give me another thought."

"Bye, Max," she said, her voice purring, her eyes twinkling. "Just in case you need more cranberry juice, I'm here Tuesday through Saturday, six to midnight."

"Nice to know," I said. I may have grinned stupidly before I turned away.

I STOOD NEXT TO THE PIANO AND WAITED FOR MAXIMUM JOE TO finish "Stormy Weather." He was almost whispering the song, but his voice was still full of warmth and pathos. When he finished the last lyric about how it was "'rainin', 'rainin all the damn time," I took out my wallet and put a twenty-dollar bill in the glass jar on the piano.

"Thank you, my good man," Joe said. "I appreciate it."

"I like the way you play and your voice. Really stirs the emotions."

"I think that was Selma." His mouth curved into a mischievous smile.

I laughed. "Yeah," I said. "Hey, you know a piano player name of Q?"

"Oh my god, sure. Q and I go way-way back. He's the best old piano hand in San Francisco, save for me of course." He laughed and his eyes flashed. "You a friend of his?"

"Yes. I like to think so. He helped me on a difficult case about a year ago."

"A case?" His smile faded. "Are you a cop?"

"No. I just help people out with problems sometimes."

"These serious problems?" he asked, pressing his lips together.

"Mostly."

He nodded, looked down at his hands as they moved across the keys together, improvising a melodic riff.

"So that twenty dollars is for me to answer some questions," he said, matter-of-factly.

"No. I really liked the song."

"Maybe that's true. But you also want to ask me for something." He raised his face toward me, sizing me up.

I grinned sheepishly and held up my hands. "Okay. You got me. I just have a couple of questions about a guy that comes in here fairly regularly, I think."

"Fred and Randy don't like it. Telling tales on customers."

"That's not what I want. This man has disappeared, and his family is very worried about him. I'm just checking out the places he was last seen, trying to put together a road map to where he might have gone."

His aimless riffing morphed into a jazzy interpretation of Paul Simon's "Homeless" from the Graceland album.

"His name is Bobby." I gave him the same description I'd given Selma and added how worried sick his daughter and brother were.

Maximum Joe kept on playing, swaying his head to the notes.

I took out two more twenty-dollar bills and put them in his jar and wondered what I was doing. I should know myself by now. I had to stop. I had to—

"I appreciate the tip, but you don't need to pay me to answer your question." Joe had his eyes closed now and a beatific smile on his face. When he finished the song, he opened his eyes, and sadness clouded his features. "So many people are homeless now. And even lots of people who have a house feeling like it isn't really home."

He shook his head and chuckled, "Listen to me. It's the music sometimes. As much as it can uplift, it often brings the blues right here and home." He tapped his fist against his chest, his heart.

I heard him. I didn't respond.

"Anyway, I know Bobby. He's got that brother. The one who owns the big casino out on Treasure Island."

"That's him."

"He was carrying a heavy burden. I don't know if it was his brother or something else. I know his wife left him. That'll unmoor a man."

"Did he talk about that with you? Did he tell you he was in trouble?"

He continued to tickle the ivories and said, "No. It wasn't like that. Not in a place like this. Sure. He said it didn't bother him.

That he was better off without that woman. But he wasn't. No, sir. He was not."

"So he didn't mention his brother or his work at the casino?"

Joe looked up and his eyes headed straight for Selma's corner, maybe checking to see that Junior wasn't lurking about. He combed the whole club before his eyes alighted on me again and said, "That was his real problem. Last time he came in, he was a different man. It wasn't just the sadness from his lost woman. He was afraid."

"And he told you about it?"

"He'd always come over and request songs, put a few dollars in my jar. He favored Marvin Gaye and Stevie Wonder. Not Duke Ellington, but nothing wrong with that. Anyway, he pulled up a chair and asked me to play Stevie's, 'Isn't She Lovely.' Said he used to sing it to his daughter when she was a little baby. He had tears in his eyes after only a few notes. He'd had one too many drinks, which wasn't too unusual for him."

His voice trailed off as he launched into the tune, immediately recognizable. He stopped after a few verses.

"...and then he told me that there was trouble at work and he didn't know what to do. That he'd gotten into it deep by telling a woman too much and that she and her friends had taken advantage of him. I could tell he wanted to say more, the drink was loosening his lips. But he caught himself and stopped."

"You didn't ask any questions?"

"That's not what I'm here for. I'll listen, but it's not my place to get too close, too chummy with the customers. Fred and Randy don't like it, sure. But I could get away with more if I wanted. Just that I don't think it'd be good. For business or for the customers. So I listen and say a reassuring word or two. What's a piano player in a bar like this got to offer, except for the wisdom and salvation in a good song played well."

"That's no small thing, Joe."

He nodded, and I thought about one of Springsteen's lyrics proclaiming that you could learn more from a three-minute record than you ever could in school.

There was more than a little truth in that, even if you weren't a musician like Joe and me, as I still like to think of myself in my more romantic moments.

"So he never said specifically what the problem was or hinted at anything he was planning on doing about it?"

"No. But it was definitely heavy on his mind. Anyway, I told him it'd probably work out, that most things we worry about are much ado about nothing, as Mr. Shakespeare put it. He smiled and thanked me, but I could tell I hadn't eased his worry any."

I asked him if there was anything else he could think of, but he said that was the sum total of his last conversation with Bobby. I put one of my cards on top of the piano and asked him to call me if he thought of anything else or if any word of Bobby came his way. I told him I'd mention his name to Q when I next saw him, and that pleased him.

I walked away from the piano and headed for the seedy little casino's exit feeling like I had gotten nowhere much, but that I'd at least given the effort I'd promised Bobby's daughter.

Seconds later though, I realized that I'd kicked over a hornet's nest and that a bit of muss and trouble were heading my way.

SEVEN

A s I approached the exit door, a woman stood up from the blackjack table close to me and caught my eye.

She nodded, came closer, and extended her hand toward me. Surprised, I wasn't sure what she wanted, but I offered a handshake, and she slipped a piece of paper into my palm, leaned in close to my right ear, and said, "Keep moving, save the note until you're out of here. You'll find what you're looking for at that address."

She stepped around me quickly and disappeared behind a bank of slot machines opposite Selma's corner of the casino.

In the dim lighting, I'd hardly gotten a close look at her. She appeared to be around thirty, short, squat, nondescript, black hair, dark eyes, wearing a badge denoting her as an employee of Fred's Flapjack Casino by the name of Karin.

I debated whether to follow her, or her directions, but my choice was taken away by the reappearance of Randy.

He was looking at me as if I was a rat he'd found lurking in broad daylight in his home. "What do you think you're doing?" he growled.

At the same moment, I felt a presence directly behind me.

"Enjoying your fine hospitality and chatting with your friendly personnel," I tried. Butter them up first, I always say.

"Bullshit," Randy said, stroking his handlebar mustache like it was his pussycat.

"I disagree with your assessment. I was doing precisely what I stated. Of course, this being America, you have the right to your opinion."

Randy's eyes widened and his face bunched up into a snarl and he kind of leered at me while grasping and tugging at his big ugly mustache, Simon Legree-like. I don't know if it was just a tic of his, or he was trying to be intimidating, or he mistook me for an Uncle Tom, but any which way, I couldn't help but laugh.

"Jeez, Randy you're cracking me up."

"Ted," Randy said.

Two big hands dropped onto my shoulders like brick claws.

Alas, their contact was brief. I reached up and back and dug my nails deep into the tops of his hands. Fortunately, I hadn't clipped them in a while, and as I scrambled for purchase, I could tell I was drawing pay dirt, or, more precisely, blood. That was confirmed by the little scream that emanated from Ted, whom I hadn't had the pleasure of meeting let alone seeing.

His big brawny mitts dropped away like bear cubs snatched from their momma.

I spun and got my first look at him. He was holding his hands, palms toward me, in front of his eyes, and his face was a mask of pain and incredulity. He looked at me and shook his head back and forth like a big old Clydesdale, which he faintly resembled.

I waited for him to neigh.

Instead, his brow furrowed, his nostrils flared, and I expected him to paw the gaudy carpet with his hooves. He dropped his hands and clenched them. "You fight like a girl."

I wasn't offended. I knew some pretty tough girls.

Behind me, I could feel Randy tense up, preparing to make his move. I pivoted and feinted toward him, putting up my fists. That startled him, and he pedaled back. I smiled and turned back to Ted.

"I have to warn you, that was only the tiniest glimpse of my girlish moves. Wait until you see how I can scratch and claw."

That did it. Ted, all close to three hundred flabby muscled pounds of him, lunged. I sidestepped but left my right foot in harm's way, just enough to hook around his left ankle. He toppled like a bowling pin, and I placed the same foot against his neck and applied appropriate pressure until he was gasping for breath while I took hold of his left arm and yanked it up so his whole body was kind of caught in a weird and painful facsimile of a bow and arrow.

Marsh had taught me the move a while back, calling it the Broken Arrow, which didn't really give a proper representation, but the hold itself was decisively incapacitating.

I pulled him to and fro for a few telling seconds, eliciting his complete cooperation.

Randy had disappeared, probably looking for reinforcements. I doubted he'd find them in a place like this. This wasn't Pirate's Cove where Poe could call on a couple of dozen men and women, each more formidable than poor Ted.

I looked down at him and said, "You'll be a good boy now?"

He didn't answer; I don't think he could, but I interpreted the look in his eyes as a resounding yes.

I released him from the Broken Arrow and quickly made my escape.

EIGHT

When I got outside, two cops were helping Robert, the homeless guy, into their police car.

I felt like a good Samaritan. I told myself I was a narcissistic asshole.

But that seems in vogue now, so I went with it.

I slipped the note from Karin from my hand to my shirt pocket without looking at it and saddled up on my motorcycle.

I thought it best to drive a safe distance from Fred's casino before reading the note and deciding what to do, just in case Randy had called the authorities on me. I doubted he would but wanted to get out of Dodge just in case.

I pulled into a small strip mall parking lot fronting a 7-Eleven, a pizza place, a chiropractor's office, and a palm reader's studio. I thought about finding out what my immediate future held but decided to let it be a surprise.

I retrieved the note and read its short and to the point content: *Beachside Motel*, 47th Street & Noriega.

It was in the Outer Sunset. Near Saint Ignatius College Prep, one of the city's finest high schools, a Jesuit establishment, although I wasn't sure how many true Jesuits were represented there anymore.

I stared at the name of the motel and the address for a few moments, trying to decide what to do. I should move on, go home, and help Alexandra pack and get ready for our trip tomorrow. I could let Marsh or one of his men check it out, and if he found Bobby or some clues where he was or what had happened, then I could turn it over to Poe, or the police, or let fate have its way.

But what the hell. It was still only late afternoon. Plenty of time tonight to get ready for Hawaii and to coordinate everything with Alexandra.

It'd only take me a few minutes to check it out and be on my way. No matter what I found, I wouldn't get involved. I'd let others handle it from there.

As I passed Devil's Teeth Baking Company on Noriega, I realized I'd been there once before with Frankie, who loved their New Orleans beignets. They were mighty fine French donuts dusted with powdered sugar. As I drove the Ducati slowly by, I could smell the scent of sourdough bread and a hint of sweetness in the air, and I thought after I visited the motel that I'd stop and get a greasy bag of beignets to give to Frankie.

She was trying to put on a good face, but I knew she wasn't happy about us leaving her, even though she'd be staying with Dao and Meiying, who she loved. In the two years she'd been living with Alexandra, it was the first time we'd left her alone for more than an overnight.

The donuts would help a little, but I knew she'd miss Alexandra, who she treated as her own mother even though she never called her that.

Maybe she'd even miss my narcissistic ass a little.

The Beachside Motel was not beside the beach, but it was near the Great Highway across the street from Ocean Beach and the great big blue Pacific.

I used to go to the submarine races, as parking and petting, back in the day, at one of the little parking alcoves off the highway fronting the beach. My first girlfriend and I spent many a late evening, panting and pawing, tussling and pleading (I believe that was mostly me) our respective cases, and exchanging gestures of affection there. She was a good Catholic girl, and I was supposed to be a good Catholic boy.

But propriety had a tendency to fly out the window in the hothouse heat of my 1985 Dodge Charger's steamy interior.

Her name was Annie Oakley. The car, not the girl. I named her after my favorite white plastic shotgun when I was a young boy.

You call me a sissy at your own peril.

But the girl was a lovely, sweet innocent who I felt guilty to the bone of fouling with my rancid lust.

I'd really swallowed the Kool-Aid that the Church provided as a salve for foregoing Eve's temptations.

But, guilty or not, deeper urges overwhelmed us both.

Golden days.

The Beachside was a weathered two-story faded blue stucco building. There were twenty-four identical units in all. I was sure each had a television on a cheap wood wall mount and a Magic Fingers vibrating bed that you could feed quarters into for fifteen minutes of shaky fun.

A well-dressed middle-aged man was behind a shiny new Formica-topped reception desk in the small but tidy office. A room deodorizer delivered a minty scent that almost hid the underlying Lysol and ammonia residues.

He greeted me with a warm smile. His small brown eyes twinkled behind large black eyeglasses. His gold-hued plastic name tag read, Frank.

"Can I help you, sir?"

"I hope so. I'm looking for someone."

"Well, we have rooms available," he responded pleasantly, but off point.

"I'm sure you do. And the next time I need one, I'll be sure to remember that. Right this moment though, it's important for me to find a gentleman I believe is a guest of yours."

The smile on his face stayed fixed, his eyes stayed twinkling. Life and its challenges seemed to amuse him.

"I'd like to help, sir, but I'm afraid that our guests' privacy is of primary concern."

Everything about Frank argued that he would do well at a much fancier establishment, and I wondered what the hell a guy like him was doing in a dump like this. I thought about inquiring more about his life's journey, but my own path beckoned more strongly.

"His name is Bobby Fenderdale."

"Sir, I understand but—"

"Just nod your chin if he's staying here. You don't have to say yes. Or maybe wink your right eye. That'll work too. No muss. No fuss."

He laughed.

I liked Frank. He was a rarity among motel desk clerks, a man with a bit of class and a sense of how strange and funny life is.

I noticed no nod nor wink.

I pushed a cards across the desk toward him, one that represented an alter ego, a pseudonym, and he picked it up and read it and then looked up at me with a quizzical expression. I understood, like all my cards, it was devoid of information save for a name and phone number.

"I do private consulting work. And my client, in this case, is the daughter of Mr. Fenderdale. She's worried about him. He's disappeared, and she fears he may harm himself." I paused, let that sink in, and then added, "I'd hate to have him harm to himself here at the Beachside Motel."

Frank studied my face, searching for something.

"Truth?" he said.

"God's honest."

Did I see a wink?

I did.

FRANK LED ME TO ROOM 12, THE END UNIT ON THE FIRST FLOOR, and knocked politely three times.

Gauging by the number of cars parked in front of the rooms, there weren't more than a handful of rentals. Despite Frank's hospitality, the place had seen better days.

The creak of someone getting up from a bed inside, then a couple of heavy steps and a brushing hand on the door. I felt eyes on us from the other side of the peephole.

The door opened a crack, to the width of the attached chain lock. An unshaven face appeared, tired, blinking eyes in the semi-bright light.

Bobby had just woken up, and he looked the worse for wear, like an extra in a Hollywood zombie film.

"Mr. Fenderdale, sorry to disturb you, but a man is here to see you."

Bobby squinted, frowned, looked over Frank's shoulder, and found me.

I didn't ring an immediate bell. He looked confused. "I'm not..." he mumbled.

"Paula sent me," I said, softly.

"What?"

"Your daughter, Bobby. You remember me, don't you? Max Plank?"

He closed his eyes and sighed. "Paula?" he said. "How did she… how did you…"

"I just want to talk for a few minutes. Paula is very worried."

"Is that okay with you, Mr. Fenderdale?" Frank asked, his voice gentle, concerned.

Bobby stood there looking lost for another twenty seconds or so and then he reached up and released the chain link.

NINE

F rank let us be, and I joined Bobby inside.

He sat on one of the double beds, his hands in his lap, his eyes to the floor.

If he was using coke, he hadn't had a hit for a while.

I sat nearby on a chair with a rickety leg.

The room was outfitted in standard circa 1970s decor—shag carpeting, particle board furnishings, the Magic Fingers, flowered print bedspreads, faded watercolor painting of a family at the beach replete with a beach ball and sand bucket. All the classics of yesteryear. The owners were fond of nostalgia or perhaps short of funds.

"How is Paula?" he murmured, not looking at me.

"She's worried about you. She told me about your problem."

"I don't want her involved. She can't be. It's too..."

"Too what?"

"They'll kill me and..."

"Who?"

"Damn it," he muttered. "Did Paula really ask you to find me?"

"Your brother did first. But I said no. Paula convinced me to try it."

"I don't see how you found me. I didn't tell..." His voice trailed off as a thought occurred to him.

"You went to Fred's casino. You found Karin. Jesus. She promised not to tell anyone." He got up, went to a little counter near the bathroom, and fiddled with a coffee machine. He tore open a packet, put it in place, and pressed the brewer button. "You want coffee?"

"I'll take whatever's left after you get yours."

He came back and sat down on the bed as the coffee maker burst into a loud pop, snap, and crackle. It sounded like Rice Krispies on amphetamines.

"Karin's nice," he murmured. "She was nice. I invited her here after we went to the movies. First time I'd been out of this dump for four days. We talked. That was stupid."

"What are you doing here? You can't hide out forever. Maybe I can help."

"How can anyone—" He stopped. His eyes bounced around the room.

I didn't know how much he knew about me. But he'd met Marsh and knew the kinds of things I consulted on. We'd chatted occasionally, and I remember him being interested, thinking what I did was pretty exciting.

It was. But you had to be a wee bit crazy, and a tad infused with a Dionysian spirit.

"Tell me," I said.

He shook his head and muttered, "Nobody can help. It's too late. They'll kill me if they find me. And worse yet. And if they don't, my brother will. I know him. I've been sitting here thinking for the past few days, and there's no way out. Except one. Do everybody a favor."

"Have you been using?" I asked.

He closed his eyes, plunged his thumb and forefinger into them, and his face cracked, threatening to break into a sob. But with a long draw of breath, he recovered. He sighed. "I ran out. Maybe that's it. Use the rest of my money and buy a dose that'll make all this go away."

I didn't think he was imminently suicidal. He was talking about it too much. But I played his game. "What about Paula? She'll be devastated. She loves you, Bobby. Think about her."

He closed his eyes as the coffee machine sputtered into an uneasy silence. He rose, filled up his cup, poured in two packets of sugar and one of powdered milk.

I followed him, filled a paper cup with the remains, and kept it black. I like a little half-and-half but refuse to put powdered chemicals into my coffee, primarily because they taste like powdered chemicals.

When we settled back down, he downed a big gulp and, with a weary melancholy in his voice, said, "That's the only thing that's stopped me. My daughter. She's always had faith in me even when I didn't deserve it, which is mostly."

I waited, sipping the weak brew. I reached out and tapped him on his knee and said, "Tell me everything, Bobby. It's your only chance."

"Damn it," he said. "I'm a coward." He lifted his paper cup up and downed the rest of the coffee and then, slowly, hesitantly, told me the story.

It surprised me how little he knew, but I guess it shouldn't have.

He hadn't known most of the people involved in the scams and didn't realize the extent of the sting while it was going on.

Only afterward, when Poe filled him in before his brother

realized that Bobby was involved, did he understand the scale of the operation.

And he didn't even understand the methods they used to steal from Pirate's Cove. How they did what they did.

It was likely that only the conspirators knew the extent and precise details of the fraud.

Poe probably knew most of it and was already hunting the violators down.

Bobby knew that cheating was going on.

And shockingly, he let it happen.

And actively aided in the theft.

TEN

Her name was Jewel.

And Jewel Allen, which Bobby now thought wasn't her real name, had a story.

Bobby was involved with lots of women. On the face of it, that seemed unlikely. He was a schlumpy character, flabby, out of shape, hapless. But maybe his perplexed, boyish demeanor appealed to a certain kind of woman. I doubted they all slept with him, but many probably felt sorry for him, harbored delusions of saving him.

I'm being too harsh. Sometimes a woman saves a man, despite the overuse of the cliché in fiction.

Bobby met Jewel when she was a blackjack dealer at Fred's casino. When he mentioned that, I immediately asked, "Could Karin be working with Jewel? That makes little sense since she sent me here, but..." I stopped, thinking about the implications.

"No. No way. Karin started after Jewel quit. I talked to Karin about Jewel. They've never met."

That made me feel a little better, like the odd stroke of luck, a stranger guiding me directly to Bobby, could be just that and not part of some larger conspiracy.

Bobby told me he never played casino games, but one day he was eating the breakfast special at Fred's Flapjack Casino and noticed Jewel, who was behind a blackjack table not far away. There was hardly anyone else around, so they got to talking.

One thing led to another.

The next night he took her out to dinner, and they ended up back at her apartment and in her bed where she told him her sad story.

She wasn't making enough money. Her mother was sick and didn't have health insurance, and Jewel was supporting the both of them on the meager pay at Fred's. Big tippers were nonexistent, and business was down.

Bobby asked her why she hadn't applied for a job at Pirate's Cove. They were always looking for experienced dealers, the pay was better, and there were whales, big spenders, and tippers, aplenty.

But there was a problem, and Jewel had been honest about it. She'd served some time in prison. She made no excuses. She'd been involved with a guy who did drugs, and he disappeared and the police showed up at his apartment, where she was living, and found a stash of heroin and cocaine. They sentenced her to two years, and she served nine months at the Central California Women's facility in Chowchilla.

Despite the catchy name, Jewel did not enjoy her time there.

She knew there was no way a casino like Pirate's Cove would hire a convicted felon and so, although her dream was to work there, she'd never dared apply.

It sounded like her story made Bobby trust her almost as much as his time in bed with her did.

I'll cut to the chase because Bobby's story meandered with lots of unnecessary detail.

Jewel's affections flattered and softened him up over the following weeks, and eventually—Bobby wasn't even sure whether it was his idea or hers—he told her that his brother owned the casino and he could hire anybody he wanted.

And he wanted her.

After she'd been hired and working there a few weeks, she continued to complain about her mother's hospital bills for cancer and how her landlord was threatening to throw her out on her ass. After they'd make love, she'd whisper in Bobby's ear about how rich his brother was and how little in comparison poor Bobby was paid, how little respect he got around the casino.

Which was all true. Everybody knew that the only reason he was working there was that he was the boss's younger brother.

He was kind of a joke at the casino, and he knew it.

Then one night, while they were making out, Jewel reached into her nightstand and removed a small packet of white powder. She said she hardly ever used the stuff, but she still had a fair stash from her ex-boyfriend that the police hadn't found.

She sprinkled a little of the magic powder into the shadowy cleft between her breasts and asked him if he'd ever snorted cocaine in that sweet spot.

Bobby said he hadn't.

She said you only live once and drew his face down into her cleavage.

ELEVEN

E verything sped up after that. It all seemed like a fantasy to Bobby, a blur of sensation and excitement and living on the edge.

And lots of fear.

He knew his brother.

He knew what his brother would do to him if he found out.

But the cocaine put a nice glow on everything.

Jewel explained that with a little help from him, a little information about security and the pit bosses and where the cameras were, that it would only take her a couple of weeks to skim off enough money to take care of all her mother's cancer treatments, and then there'd be plenty left over for her and Bobby to escape to a Caribbean island where no one would ever find them.

It was a plan only a hapless cokehead could find plausible.

But he was jealous of Poe. He felt that he deserved more. He was tired of being taken for a chump.

Jewel was exciting, like nobody else he'd ever met, and he wanted to run away with her.

He wanted more titty hits.

So, with a queasy feeling in the pit of his stomach, he agreed.

Over the following days, he observed operations at the casino with a more studied, purposeful eye. He asked questions he'd never bothered with before, trying to make them seem innocent, just an employee, the boss's brother, trying to understand more about how things ran and how they kept all that money safe.

No one suspected a thing, Bobby thought.

But, after Bobby disappeared and the scams came to light, security personnel and pit bosses went to Poe and hesitantly recounted his recent and out of character queries.

At Jewel's blackjack table, Bobby ran interference, just like she'd taught him. Putting his body in front of the security cameras on her hands at just the right moment. Creating the occasional disturbance by glad-handing a customer or spilling a drink. Nothing too obvious or too frequent.

Jewel was a pro, and she didn't need much help.

What Bobby didn't know at the time was that she had "associates" working with her, accomplices posing as players, sitting at her blackjack table, and an elaborate signaling system allowing them to know when to hold them and when to fold them.

He also was unaware that one of the pit bosses was in collusion with her, and there was theft going on at the baccarat tables, the slots, and even the roulette tables, where someone used an electronic device to change the rotation of the spinning silver ball.

Everything was going smoothly, according to plan.

Jewel said they had over three-quarters of a million dollars.

It was almost time to pull out. Make their escape.

AND THEN, EARLY ONE WICKED COLD SATURDAY NIGHT, WITH THE fog rolling over the Golden Gate Bridge like a harbinger, Jewel came home.

Bobby wasn't supposed to be there.

But he'd bought a ring.

He had it in a box, and the box was in his hand, and the hand was in the little loft you got to with foldaway stairs, just like with the bunk bed he'd slept in as a child. The loft was tiny. Jewel used it for storage—mainly suitcases and extra pillows and clothes on a hanger rack.

He was up there hiding, ready to give her the biggest surprise of her life.

But she beat him to it.

SHE WASN'T ALONE.

Not nearly.

There were four men with her, and Bobby knew two.

What they said in the next half-hour while he crouched above them, quiet as a mouse, astounded him.

But he could have dealt with that. They could have talked it out.

He'd still give her the ring.

But what Jewel said about him, while the box in his hand got heavier and heavier, while his fingers curled around it and tightened and tightened until the four sides of it collapsed, devastated him.

He tried to be the mouse. He felt like a mouse, and he hated that feeling.

He knew that he was a rat. He'd betrayed his brother who'd taken a chance on him.

He was a chump. He'd always been a chump.

He found himself crying, and then he heard a sound and realized he'd let out a sob.

Suddenly the voices down below quieted.

Which was a relief because he didn't think he could bear another word from Jewel's sweet, treacherous lips.

THEY WANTED TO KILL HIM.

Jewel was all for it.

That was the worst.

That's when he wished, at that moment, that they go ahead and do it.

But they were afraid. They weren't murderers. That wasn't part of the plan.

So they made him promise that he wouldn't tell anyone what he knew.

Especially his brother.

He promised. He was numb.

He felt like his life was over.

They argued for a while. Could they trust him? They needed insurance, and that's when Jewel mentioned his daughter, Paula.

She knew what the girl meant to him.

So they told him if they found out he ever betrayed them, told anyone who they were, they would go after Paula.

And that's why, even after everything he told me, Bobby refused to divulge the names of the men who were Jewel's accomplices.

TWELVE

I would find out, one way or another.
But, after he'd talked himself out, I could see he was
exhausted.

I could tell that he wanted, needed, a hit of something strong,
something that would take him away from that little room and the
memories of his lost love, his shattered illusions.

I could tell how scared he was for his daughter.

She was the only thing he had left.

If he put her in harm's way, he had nothing to live for.

I just had to convince him we could keep Paula safe.

I thought the bad guys were just bluffing and that once Poe
had their names, they wouldn't be able to hurt anyone ever again.

But I didn't press him right away.

I asked him what he was doing there at the Beachside Motel,
lovely idyll that it was.

He said that after that terrible night when they'd threatened
his daughter, Jewel had disappeared, and he hadn't seen her or the
others since.

Maybe she'd made it to that Caribbean island without him.

He needed time to think. And he was afraid that the guys who threatened his daughter might reconsider and come back to get him. He knew his brother was looking for him, and he didn't want to face Poe.

His shame was a bigger factor than his fear of what his brother might do to him.

He said that Karin was the only person who knew where he was. But now that she'd betrayed his confidence, no matter her intentions, he needed to move.

But he was running out of money, and he was tired.

Tired of everything.

I understood. And I also knew that it was the cocaine, or lack of it, that was helping drain his energy and will, amping the desperation.

I told him to take a nap. That I'd get dinner for us and we'd talk more when I got back.

He sighed and laid back on the bed and closed his eyes.

As I opened the motel room door, he called out, "I need to see my daughter. I need to see Paula." He was up on his elbows, his eyes suddenly wide, urgent. "Tonight. We can—"

I closed the door, came back inside, sat beside him on the bed. "Why?" I asked.

"She's smart. She's the only one I trust. She'll know what I should do, even if I don't like it." He went to the dresser beneath the TV and retrieved his cell phone. He picked it up, swept his finger across the screen, whispering, "My baby," as he tapped her number in.

She took less than twenty minutes to get there, and when she did, it shocked me to the bone.

They had set me up.

Led me like a puppet on a string.

And I had no idea why.

THIRTEEN

The Paula Fenderdale who showed up at the Beachside Motel wasn't the same Paula who came to my boat that morning.

Bobby insisted the stranger standing in front of us was his daughter.

And, oddly enough, the stranger, the sweet woman with the puzzled expression on her face said she'd known Bobby, her father, all of her twenty-nine years.

The real Paula was wide-hipped, like the imposter who'd hired me, but she had dirty blond hair instead of brown, a long aquiline nose instead of a pug number, and she was three or four inches taller, and at least a half-decade younger.

Bobby and his daughter were concerned and confused about who might have been impersonating Paula, but they were even more focused on solving Bobby's current dilemma.

I listened absently, but my mind was whirling back over my conversation with the oh-so-credible imposter who'd come to my boat and, with a performance that had my vote for Best

Supporting Actress in a Comedy/Drama, convinced me to go looking for Bobby Fenderdale.

It made no sense.

Something so planned, calculated, outrageous, and dangerous had to have a motive. And a damn important one.

I hated being played. More troubling, something was going on behind the scenes that was profoundly unsettling and likely hazardous to the wellbeing of everyone in the room, including me.

I had the feeling that unless I figured something out and real soon, we were all in a heap of trouble.

My thoughts drifted, and I heard Paula say, "Daddy, go to Uncle Poe. Don't worry about me. He'll protect me, protect us. He'll forgive you."

Bobby had already summarized the whole story, leaving out some details it was best a man's daughter not hear.

Snorting cocaine from between a woman's breasts was never mentioned.

They argued for a while. She sat on the bed next to her father, holding his hands, looking into his eyes. I tried to stay out, let them talk. I made another pot of coffee and shared it all around.

I called the number that phony Paula had given me. It went to voice mail with a robotic message. I thought about calling Marsh to see if he'd made any progress on the background check I'd requested on the woman but realized he wouldn't have come up with anything other than the assumedly mundane information on the real deal. I hadn't given him a picture of the woman who'd tried to hire me, not being in the habit of taking snapshots of my clients.

I might have to rethink my protocol.

I called Alexandra and told her I'd be home late. It annoyed her that I had made myself so scarce right before we were scheduled to leave. I apologized and told her I'd be home as soon as possible. I didn't go into the complexities I was confronting.

"Famous last words," she said.

I guess I hung up after that without responding. I called Marsh and left a message telling him we needed to pow wow.

Back in the motel room, I found both of them in tears.

I made more coffee.

I stood near the bathroom waiting for the caffeine express to stop its racket.

"Daddy told me everything. He told me who did this. We've decided to go see Poe," Paula said, after blowing her nose. Bobby sat silently, teary-eyed, a hangdog expression on his face.

"That's probably a good idea. He'll find you anyway, eventually."

"Can you come with us, Mr. Plank? Daddy says you told him that his brother tried to hire you to find him. That means he must trust you. That you're good at what you do."

I didn't know if Poe trusted me, or anyone else, but even if he did, I didn't want to run interference.

"Daddy thinks you'll do a better job explaining it all to him. He doesn't think he can do it. He'll break down and make a mess of it."

I wanted to say no. Me being there would likely piss Poe off.

Bobby had to man up.

But, I knew Paula was right. Her father would probably screw it all up and get the worst possible reaction.

"I'll consider it, only if you tell me who Jewel's accomplices were and everything you know about them." I looked from Bobby to Paula. It seemed more vital now, after finding out how I'd been duped, that I get every bit of information he had.

Then, out of the blue, a realization hit me like a revelation from on high.

I couldn't believe it hadn't been the first thought when the real Paula showed up.

"Bobby, describe Jewel."

He twisted his mouth to one side in puzzlement.

"What does she look like? Describe her as best you can."

He described to a tee the woman who came to my boat with such a convincing story and performance.

Which made me feel better because it made perfect sense. But that feeling didn't last long.

How had she found me?

How did she find out about Poe trying to hire me?

That thought brought up so many new questions it made my head spin like a dreidel.

Was Poe involved more deeply than he'd let on? Was someone inside his organization still tied to Jewel and her accomplices?

Was Jewel using me to find Bobby because she was worried that he'd disappeared and might go back on his promise, despite the danger to his daughter?

I had the feeling that there was more here than any of that. But untangling it with so few facts seemed impossible.

I needed to be alone to think. I needed to brainstorm with Marsh, tease out the possibilities into likelihoods.

Most of all I needed to find Jewel Allen.

And I might have to start back at Pirate's Cove, in Poe's lair, as it had all started there—the initial scams and the plot to involve me in all of this.

So maybe going with Bobby and Paula to see the big boss was the right move, after all.

It was then I realized I'd probably lost fifteen hundred dollars and incurred the wrath and disappointment of my woman once again.

I wasn't going to Hawaii.

Bobby mumbled his response to my demand for more information. "Right. Sure. But God, I'm hungry. Can we get some dinner, and I'll tell you while we're eating? The place right across the street," he mumbled, waving with his hand to point toward a Chinese joint within sight of the motel.

I didn't want to wait another second. But he was a man about to burst or break. That wouldn't help anyone.

Bobby wanted Beef Chow Mein and Egg Foo Young. Paula didn't care.

Neither did I. I told them I'd be back in twenty minutes.

It wouldn't hurt to give father and daughter a little time alone.

Bobby said he couldn't face his brother that night. He was too fried.

Paula said she'd stay with him and they'd go together in the morning.

I thought about whether they'd be safe there for the night.

I thought about calling Marsh to send a man to watch over them but decided against it. After dinner, I'd go home and explain things to Alexandra, hope that she still liked me enough not to dump me like yesterday's leftovers.

Then I'd come back and watch over them. I was still confounded about Jewel's intentions and afraid that she and the other thieves might be desperate enough to show up out of the blue.

I couldn't help but feel it was on me to make sure that father and daughter remained safe for one more night.

FOURTEEN

I jogged the roughly fifty yards across the street and ordered. Like most Chinese restaurants, the Jade Dragon was a deceptively popular place. Only an elderly couple sat silently at one of the nine plastic-topped tables inside, but there was a constant flow of people picking up takeout.

The place was tiny, cramped, loaded with Asian tchotchkes from plastic jade plants to multicolored fans to photos of cuddly panda bears.

The lobby in front had a red vinyl couch that looked back on the road and the motel. I stood with my back to the counter where a half dozen authentic Asians busily cooked, packaged, rang up orders, and chattered incomprehensibly.

While I waited, I kept an eye on the motel. The Beachside looked forlorn and spooky in the shadowy pall cast by dull overhead street lighting. A crescent moon halfway up the sky peeked out between black and gray clouds drifting low.

While I watched absently, I thought about how Jewel Allen had known, because I'd told her, that I had only less than a day, a few hours at most, to look for Bobby.

She may have known that before she came to visit me.

Did that mean she knew that was all it would take for me to find him?

Which argued for the possibility she already knew where Bobby was and directed me right toward him using Karin at Fred's casino, despite what Bobby had said about the fact that they were strangers to each other.

And perhaps, although it seemed improbable, with an assist from the owner, Leslie, at the gym.

The more I thought about it, the more perplexing and impossible to fathom the whole affair seemed.

As I tried to piece all the fragments of the past day together to make it fit into a more coherent pattern, the door to Room 12 opened and a dark figure who was not Bobby or his daughter stepped out, closed the door, paused for a moment, looking out to the street, toward me, and then moved to the side of the building and disappeared behind the motel.

My heart stutter-stepped, and I rushed out of the restaurant with the cry of "Mister? Mister! Your food is ready!" echoing in my ears.

I raced across the street and through the parking lot, veering past the edge of the motel, following the track of the shadow. I pulled up to find a shallow, dry creek bed, tall grass, a line of elm trees, and an empty horizon. I stood still, scanning the entire area, looking for the slightest movement.

Nothing.

The dark shadow had disappeared.

The figure leaving Room 12 had been fully dressed in black, with a hoodie covering its head.

I had seen no facial features. It was just too dark and far away.

But something in the way the shadow moved, the tilt of the head, the grace of the movements, immediately brought a name to mind.

I couldn't be sure. It was just a feeling, but I would have bet a nice, clean one-hundred-dollar bill I was right.

I was out of breath. I felt my heart hammering my chest, herky-jerky, as I thought about the fact that if I was on the money about the identity of the intruder, then everything I'd been thinking was wrong.

The intruder.

I dashed back to the room, threw the door open, stepped inside.

Bobby lay across the bed at an odd angle, his head lolling over one side of the mattress. One of his eyes was missing.

Every other moment, a drop of blood spilled from that void in his face and made the large black stain on the shag carpeting beneath him that much larger.

I turned to rush back out and continue my search for the shadowy intruder, and, at the same time, felt more than heard a rustling motion and glimpsed pale flesh and a black object filling the space in front of my face.

I fell, the floor rushing toward me fast and final.

An explosion burst in my head, along with a deep cratering darkness.

I felt my body spasm and then I felt nothing.

FIFTEEN

I t was dark, and I was floating, hovering in a dreamscape, somewhere vast and strange. There were stars in the swirling black clouds above me, and I was part of them.

I thought nothing for a long time until I realized that my eyes were closed.

When I opened them, there were no stars or clouds or black sky, or maybe there were, but I wasn't seeing them.

I was staring at a stained popcorn ceiling.

I wondered how old the ceiling was and if it was riddled with asbestos and whether the exposure might make me sick at some future time.

My thoughts were a jumble, as was my place in space and time.

My eyes closed again, and when they opened, I was still staring at that ugly ceiling, but this time I knew where I was.

A room, number twelve, at the Beachside Motel.

All of it came rushing back in a moment's exhalation. And it made me sick. I rolled over, lunged to the corner of the bed, and vomited all over the floor.

I felt better after that until I registered that I'd vomited onto a large dark spot on the carpet below me. I glanced sideways and found Bobby's face still hanging in mid-air, still missing an eye.

A series of sharp smells assaulted me—rotting meat, cheap perfume, shit.

Bobby had soiled his pants.

I wretched again but didn't throw up. I made it to my feet and stumbled away from the bed and into the bathroom to look at myself.

I examined my face and head in the dirty mirror. I felt beneath my hair. A large bump swelled painfully on the rear right back of my skull. A purple bruise darkened the right side of my face, and my ear looked like a discolored, misshapen hammerhead. Max Weinberg was taking a break from his duties with the E Street Band to pound drums inside of my head like some mad demon.

I was probably in need of a concussion protocol.

But that would have to wait.

I had to get out of that room. But before I stumbled out, a thought occurred to me.

Where was Paula?

At the same moment, I looked at the flowered curtain hanging from a faded golden rod pulled across the bathtub to my right.

My stomach roiled and retched.

I drew the curtain back.

Paula lay sprawled at the bottom of the tub, her mouth curled into a surprised rictus. A small, black, jagged hole lay just below her hairline.

A pool of blood encircled her hair.

I stumbled out of the bathroom and looked at Bobby on the bed and then back at Paula.

What had I allowed to happen to these two poor souls?

SIXTEEN

Ten minutes before midnight.

When I'd re-entered the motel after my visit to the Jade Dragon, it had been a little after 8 p.m.

I'd been out for almost three hours.

Why was I still alive while Bobby and Paula had been eliminated as threats?

And to whom?

I couldn't get the notion, the near-certain feeling, that I knew who the shadowy figure I'd seen outside the room was.

Poe's Angelique.

His right hand, a trained killer. A pro.

I couldn't believe that this was how Poe would take care of his brother and his innocent niece.

Poe was guilty of a lot of things, but this seemed beyond the pale, even for him.

More likely, Jewel and her accomplices had acted out of desperation, of fear, not of the police, but of what Poe would unleash if Bobby told his brother who they were.

They could run, but eventually, one way or the other, Poe

would find them and teach them a lesson that other fools could learn from.

You don't mess with Poe or his endeavors ever.

Without having seen the dark figure outside the room, I would have had to blame the casino thieves—Jewel and her gang gone mad.

And even now, I thought there had to be an explanation for Angelique's presence, if it had truly been her, other than murderous intent.

But maybe she was just on my mind since I'd seen her yesterday and I was imagining things. Could the figure who disappeared behind the motel have stepped back into the room in time to knock me out?

It seemed improbable. Could she have circled around and gotten inside through the little bathroom window that looked out over the gully in back of the motel?

Impossible.

If Angelique had been there, maybe Poe just had her following me, hoping to find Bobby, or help me if I ran into any trouble.

But, if it wasn't Poe and Angelique, and the casino thieves had tracked Bobby here, if my own visits to the gym and the casino had led them here, then they couldn't be sure that Bobby hadn't told me everything he knew.

Keeping me alive was too much of a risk.

Had they thought I was dead?

They would have checked my pulse. And put a bullet in my head just like poor Paula.

I was sitting in a chair pressed against the wall, as far as I could get from Bobby's stench. I had a wet hand towel from the bathroom pressed over my nose and mouth.

My stomach roiled, and I struggled to keep any remaining contents down.

I had to call the police. Or Marsh? Or Poe? Or Alexandra?

My mind wasn't working well. My thoughts flashed and crashed and dissolved into a muddle.

Damn it, Plank. This is important. Why had they left me alive?

I looked around, surveyed the room. Looked down at my hands, noticed the red and purple blotches on my fingers. On the nails. The stains on my shirt and pants.

It couldn't be.

They'd never get away with it.

If they planned this on the fly, it wouldn't work.

In any case, it wouldn't.

No one would believe it.

Well, mostly no one. There were doubters in any crowd.

And could Poe somehow be involved, either on his own, for his own nefarious purposes, or had he formed an unlikely alliance with Jewel and her gang?

I couldn't dismiss the notion, but I didn't believe it.

Poe was capable of setting me up. He had people he controlled in the police department and throughout San Francisco's circles of power.

Why?

I had a big bump on the back of my head.

I had an explanation, perfectly logical.

I was in no shape to look for evidence, to see what they had planted to make me look guilty, other than the victims' blood on my hands.

I scoured the room anyway, looking for a gun or anything else suspicious. I searched the bodies and found nothing important. My card was in Bobby's pocket. That could be explained, but I took it anyway.

I cursed myself for leaving the room before I got the names of Jewel's accomplices from Bobby. I felt guilty as hell for leaving them alone.

I had nothing. I was nowhere.

The killers had left me alive for no clear reason. They didn't know that I didn't know who they were.

My thoughts circled themselves, whirling dervishes in search of enlightenment.

Exhaustion along with a cratering migraine of pain racked my head.

Sirens wailed in the distance.

I bent over, my chest on my knees, afraid I might upchuck again.

The sirens got louder, screeching like a murder of crows, rushing closer.

I put my hands on my head trying to contain a blast of emotion.

I needed time. The sirens howled closer.

If I ran, there would be consequences.

If I stayed, there would be a grueling night of questions for which I felt not near capable. I couldn't imagine bearing it.

You don't have a choice, Max.

You can deal with this, with them. Leaving would be worse than stupid.

I have to say, in my defense, I was a little out of my mind.

But, even then, when I didn't have an inkling that the whole sordid slippery mess would come to a final resounding conclusion less than a chaotic twenty-fours later, there was a bother, a tick I could almost seize, its inflamed tip buried in my brain. Something I knew was vitally important, but that I was too damaged or dense to lock down.

I felt like I was on some weird amalgam of mind-altering substances.

It had to be the blow to my head.

It would take the police detectives time to figure out I had been there, that it involved me. I hadn't given the desk clerk, Frank, my real name.

Unless they had the outside help I was sure was coming their way, the same help that had probably brought those sirens to the Beachside Motel.

I got up, stumbled to the door, stepped outside. The strobes of flashing lights from the howling sirens lit up the street like cluster bombs from enemy aircraft.

I ran or staggered to Ruby, my bike. Frankie had named her after her blood-red color, and I liked it. I turned the key, pressed the start button, and the computer started her up for me.

I turned the throttle, lurched sideways to the back of the motel. I roared down the slope to the creek bed and came up the other side, straddling a rutted hill covered with tall grass.

What am I doing?

Where am I going?

I had the barest outline of a plan and a thought about where I had to begin, but I needed to sit down and think it through. The only way I could do that was to put as much distance between me and the Beachside Motel as possible.

It was risky, but what is life without risk?

Or was it just plain foolhardy, reckless, bold, but utterly stupid?

All of that.

I glanced backward in time to see a half dozen squad cars pulling into the parking lot.

I turned, revved the throttle, and pushed off, glancing down at Ruby's dashboard—as the digital clock clicked precisely to the witching hour.

A moment later, I disappeared behind that line of elm trees back dropping the Beachside Motel before the cops could get out of their cars.

SEVENTEEN

Things at my home, *Acapella Blues*, seemed normal, which surprised me.

I was ready for something else, expecting it, primed, operating on a razor's edge of tension after the night's shocking turn.

I approached her stealthily along the pier, surveying the surroundings with a jaundiced eye.

The boat floated peacefully, calmly, unaffected by the bad luck and trouble that had battered me, casting me adrift.

It looked like home, like a sanctuary.

I knew it wasn't. Not now.

I couldn't stay long.

In the galley kitchen, beneath the sink, I lifted out cleaning supplies and the broken fluke of an old anchor covering a rubber mat I pulled aside to access a large safe embedded beneath. I dialed the combination lock—5...19...75...AS. Alexandra's birthdate and initials.

I removed three untraceable burner smartphones and a five-figure wad of cash I kept for emergencies. I removed and loaded two pistols, a subcompact Glock 30 and a semi G29.

I don't like to carry. Don't much like the things. But I go to the firing range every month, and at times like this, they come in handy.

I also strapped on a calf holster holding a Cold Steel Leatherneck blade.

My head was still ablaze, lit with hurt and confusion, but I acted by rote, performing actions that required nothing but practiced ritual.

I activated one of the burners and called Marsh to set up a meeting and arrangements. Marsh being Marsh, I didn't have to explain a thing. He asked no questions. He knew, by my voice and manner, that something serious had gone down.

Marsh can be maddening, but at times like this, I knew how lucky, doing what I do, I was to have him as my partner and friend.

I love the guy and would do just about anything for him. I've seen what he will do for me, proving more than once that there is no limit. I've tried to match that level, but probably lack his particular unwavering ethos, the code he lives by, which puts true friendship, something he offers few, above all other values.

I moved to the cabin, sat down, closed my eyes. Tried to quiet my mind while taking stock of things.

I could start in one of two ways.

Either big or small.

Big was seductive and how I was naturally inclined by temperament.

Start with a bang. Hit hard. Shake things up. Force the truth out by attacking the head of the snake.

But this approach, particularly with the myriad uncertainties, in this case, was more than likely to blow up in my face with untold collateral damage to me and mine.

Starting smaller, slower, in accord with the tenets of the trade I am only loosely affiliated with, would take more time.

Time I didn't have.

And yet it was the prudent course, the way to be sure that when I went big, I would be operating with at least a modicum of understanding that would improve the odds of getting at some measure of the truth, if not the whole truth, so help me all great and powerful Oz.

It was just after 2 a.m.

Time for my first rendezvous.

EIGHTEEN

The rear supply door to the Kabuki theater was unlocked, and I slipped in and closed it quietly behind me. I followed a dull glow of light in the darkness to a large dressing room behind the main stage.

I found Marsh lying on a mauve yoga mat in Shavasana, or corpse pose, his eyes closed, his hands and feet open and splayed out, his face calm and relaxed.

I sat on a black stool against the back wall and closed my eyes for just a moment. When I opened them, Marsh was sitting up, his legs crossed at his ankles, his hands on his knees, alert, his attention focused powerfully on me.

I could hear nothing but the quiet solemnity of the great theater. Marsh had told me that a Kabuki theater was a place of tradition and cultural importance. He believed it should carry an almost spiritual aspect and that he wanted it to convey this sacred ritualistic tradition. He and Dao had incorporated this desire into the architecture, the design, and the materials, as natural as possible, that had been used.

Despite my addled state, I felt it. Something here conveyed a sense of history, of permanence in a sea of evanescence.

This too shall pass, I thought, nonsensically.

"Any problems?" I asked.

"None," he answered.

"Thank you."

He nodded. Waited.

I sighed and summarized the events of the past several hours.

"Shit-storm," he muttered when I concluded.

I laughed, causing a rumble of pain to wrack my skull. I winced. Then said, "And I got shit-hammered."

"Your head," he said, "should be looked at."

"You're looking."

He got up, ran his fingers gently through my hair, found the bump, traced his fingers over it, then knelt and took my face in his hands. His eyes bore into mine with focused intensity. I felt a little awkward, intimidated. He moved my face slowly back and forth, then raised a finger and told me to follow it with my eyes. I did the best I could.

He rose and returned to his yoga mat. When he'd resettled in a lotus position, he said, "Still, you should have it checked."

I pursed my lips and nodded my chin. It would have to wait, and he knew it.

"You really think it was Angelique?" he said.

"Likely. Not a hundred percent sure, but I'd bet more than a nickel on it."

"That why you bailed?"

"One reason. You think I was wrong?"

"Probably," he said, holding my eyes. "I would've done the same thing though," and then he added a refrain that we have had cause to use more than once: "Whether tis nobler in the mind to suffer the slings and arrows of outrageous fortune." He stopped.

I finished it for him. "Or to take arms against a sea of troubles."
I paused, then murmured, "And by opposing, end them."

The grim smile that passed between us fortified me.

"How long before they figure out I was there?"

He shrugged. "Could be a while, unless they have outside help,
which sounds like they will."

"Did you reach your contact?" I asked.

"He was none too happy. With the time of my call or my
request."

"Turned you down flat, eh?"

"We've got twenty-four hours, not a minute more."

That wasn't much time, but it gave me cover when the
moment came for me to explain myself to the powers that be.

"Plenty of time then," I said.

"Yes. I hear the bass are biting."

"Maybe we should wait until later in the week?"

"Spoilsport," he quipped.

"Shit-storm," I said.

"Quite," he responded and got up again, retrieved a leather
satchel, and handed it to me. Inside, I found a blond wig, a
mustache in a little plastic wrapper, a bottle of black hair dye, and
a folder with two fake driver's licenses. He handed me a set of
keys for a late model Mazda SUV, one of the more non-attention-
grabbing autos in his large collection.

I'd parked Ruby in an underground lot not far away in
Ghirardelli Square.

After I zipped the satchel closed, I looked up and said, "Why?" I
was speaking to myself as much as to my friend.

"There's the rub," he said, continuing the Shakespearean
allusions.

"If they're framing me for murder, why? If it's Jewel's gang, I
can follow the line of thinking. If Poe is involved, I don't have
a clue."

"Strange, either way. The thieves may just be trying to buy time until they disappear. And Poe's motives, as usual, are depth-less. We need to untangle the mystery enough to at least point our finger at the right target."

I nodded. "So, you'll get me enough to catch Jewel's scent any moment now?"

"Soon, if all goes well. I've got people at both casinos. Trying to be subtle at Pirate's Cove, not so much at Fred's. Hope to stir up a photo and more soon. The only luck we have is that they're open 24-7. Give me the burner number and, with any luck, you'll be able to identify her and know where to look within a few hours."

"Thanks, buddy. You know, don't you?"

Marsh looked away. "I'll be ready. 24-7, just like Fred's," he murmured, and I knew it was true.

NINETEEN

Alexandra looked beautiful with her long, auburn hair spread out around the pillow beneath her. The lavender-colored comforter was drawn up to a few inches beneath her collarbone revealing more than a glimpse of lush cleavage.

She could still take my breath away even after three years together. My heart felt as heavy as my head. For some reason, I was afraid I might lose her.

I whispered her name, "Alexandra."

Her soft breathing altered, and she stirred beneath the covers. I touched her hair with the tips of my fingers. Her eyes flashed open, a startled look on her face. "What..." She flinched in fear, found my face in the darkness, relaxed.

"Oh," she mumbled. "Max."

"Alex, I'm sorry, but we need to talk."

She frowned and said, "Now?"

I knew she thought it was about our relationship as if I'd come to discuss the state of it in the middle of the night. But if she gave it even a second thought, she'd realize that wasn't the case. I normally avoided all "relationship" talk as if it were bubonic.

Her response threw me off for a moment, and my heart sank as I realized I had no right to ask her to help me now and that she might well turn me down.

She pulled herself up into a sitting position, bringing the covers over her chest, holding it there with her hands, resting back against the green fabric headboard. "Our flight is later this morning, Max. We'll be alone for a week in Hawaii." She rubbed her eyes with her fingertips, took a deep breath, trying to shake off the sleep.

"About that."

Her forehead furrowed, and she gave me a sharp look.

"This was your idea. You insisted. It wasn't easy for me to take time off from work."

"I know," I said with an outtake of breath. "Something happened."

"Are you saying we're not going?"

"Let me explain."

She cast the covers aside and naked, overwhelmingly naked, walked to her closet and removed a white cotton bathrobe. She tossed it over her shoulders, tied the stays, and turned back to me.

"Max, please, this was a big deal for me to—"

"Babe, I don't have much time."

She sat down on the bed, her back to me.

"Please, Alex. Can you give me five minutes? I wouldn't have come here if it wasn't an emergency."

Her shoulders rose as she took a breath in, and then they fell, and that little action, the drooping of her shoulders, touched me and I felt lousy. Lousy about what had happened to Bobby and Paula, lousy about what I was about to ask of this woman I cared for so deeply, lousy about my distance from her and Frankie lately.

She turned, lifted her legs off the floor and onto the bed, wrapped her arms around her legs, and put her chin on one knee. Her eyes found mine. They were full of disappointment, or more precisely, melancholy, sadness that filled me with more of the same.

"Go ahead," she murmured, in a soft voice, like a little girl, or so it sounded, and that made me want to grab her and hold her in my arms and tell her how I felt and that I was sorry and how I would feel without her.

Altogether a whole mess of feelings I was uncomfortable with and had no time for.

So I just rambled, recounting again what had happened since I talked with her last, which seemed like a long time, but in reality, was less than a day.

She listened without reaction until I got to the discovery of the dead bodies at the motel when she looked up and said, "Max," with a horrified expression on her face.

I described the scene with a minimum of detail and then finished up with my current conflicting theories of who might be responsible for the murders and why.

"I'm so sorry," she said, when I'd finished.

"No. No reason to be. I startled you awake in the middle of the night." I paused, studied her face, which was full of concern, for me, I hoped, and for what had happened. "Look-it, babe, I know I haven't been here for you and Frankie, at least not really... emotionally lately, but, and that's why I wanted this Hawaii trip, I'm aware of it and—"

"Not now," she said, sharply. "You were right. This is an emergency. I'm still not sure why you left the motel. Even if Marsh agrees. Marsh isn't always right. In fact, he's wrong a lot. I think you should go to the police. You can explain everything. No matter if someone's trying to frame you. They won't succeed. By running you look guilty. At least in their eyes."

She got up, walked around the bed, sat beside me. Put her hand on my thigh. "I think what you're doing is a mistake. It's too dangerous. You don't know enough. Let the police handle this. I know it's not your way. That's the problem. Once you get your teeth into something like this, you never let go. Nothing else matters as much. Not me. Not Frankie." She paused, shook her head. "You're not invincible. You're just a man."

I ignored the insult and told her about Marsh's contact in the Mayor's office, a key player in politics in the city along with being involved in just about every major criminal case. He had strong connections with the top command in the police department.

"So this guy is going to protect you when the police find out that you were at the motel and your DNA is all over the bodies?"

"Not exactly." I explained what precisely would happen when the story hit the morning news.

"You're kidding."

I just looked at her.

"My God! You and Marsh are crazy."

I couldn't disagree, and it made me smile and feel a little ashamed, so I looked away from her shocked gaze.

"I don't know what to do about you, Max."

I looked at her, and there was that glint in her eye that she gets when I've disturbed and confounded her, but also engaged her, excited her, made her think I'm one of a kind and she isn't going to ever find anyone like me.

At least that's my take.

Watching her, I detected a hint of a smile she was trying to suppress and then, shaking her head as if she couldn't believe what she was about to say, she looked directly into my eyes and said, "What can I do to help?"

I curbed another smile, but inside, my chest blossomed with feeling. I reached down to the carpet where I'd placed Marsh's satchel, unzipped it, and took out the blond wig and false driver's license ID. I held them up for her in my right hand, feeling guilty as hell about what I was about to ask her to do.

Her eyes flashed as she registered the items in my hand.

I saw an opening, leaned in, and placed a soft, lingering kiss on her lips.

She let me.

TWENTY

The Pelican Inn wasn't.

An inn, that is.

An inn should be a lovely but modest little establishment along a country road, preferably with an Anglo-Saxon feel or decor, offering both comfortably humble rooms, a kindly manager-bartender, and big portions of hearty home-made food.

The Pelican had none of these, and no discernible connection to water birds other than the lopsided plastic facsimile thrust into a spot of lawn out front, but what it offered was what I needed even more: anonymity, privacy, and location.

In other words, it was cheap, took cash, and required no ID. Hardly anyone was in residence, and it was a stone's throw from where the whole damn mess had started less than a day ago— Matthew's Manufacturing Muscles and Fred's Flapjack Casino.

I needed to wait somewhere for Marsh to provide me with a trail of crumbs to follow and for the morning news to announce the murders that would shake things up, hopefully, in the bad guys' dens of iniquity.

The Pelican, a dank, faded single story motel built in the fifties that smelled of mold, rotting wood, and flowery nose-clenching air deodorizer, would suffice for my purposes.

It was a block in from 92, The El Camino Real, and about a mile from Fred's.

The thought of sleeping was difficult, but I knew it was what I needed before the upcoming journey I was bound and likely to take. My head felt like the wrong end of a block of timber under the assault of an ax man.

I normally would have taken a sitting position on the floor, but you could almost see the bacteria festering in the stained carpet, so I sat in a lotus position in the middle of the bed with my palms open on my knees and tried to relax and breathe.

After ten minutes of valiant struggle with my thoughts, the relentless interrogation of the facts of the past twenty-four hours that I was helpless to stop, I surrendered.

My mind is the only thing separating me from being the Ultimate Yogi.

Finally, exhausted, I lay back on the bed and fell asleep without realizing it.

My eyes flickered open to a familiar song of my youth—a high-pitched smother of bells running into each other.

My new phone was set to an old-fashioned ring.

When I brought it in front of my eyes, I was surprised to see that it was just after 7 a.m. I'd been asleep for almost five hours. It seemed like three minutes. I felt more enervated than refreshed.

I swiped the display open and waited. Nothing.

It had to be Marsh. I didn't recognize the number because he was using an untraceable phone too.

Still, feeling a slight paranoia, I did not speak first.

After another few seconds, Marsh said, "Jewel Allen isn't her real name."

Not a surprise.

And yet I felt my pulse quicken at the news. It meant Marsh had caught the scent of the prey or perhaps even more. It meant I could take action. It meant I could leave the Pelican Not Inn.

"You found her?" I said.

"Not exactly. How's that head of yours?"

"Hard as ever." I was lying. It felt soft and vulnerable as did the stream of consciousness running through it, but I didn't want Marsh rushing in to save me. I had to do this myself, although I would need assists from him and Alexandra.

"Glad to hear it. Hope it's not too hard to listen to reason."

"What are you talking about?"

"I doubt it'll be easy to find Jewel or to get her cooperation."

It didn't matter how easy it would be. The phrase, "Easy is as easy does," popped into my mind, but, thinking on it for a moment, I didn't have a good idea of what that even meant.

"We got nowhere with the owner at the gym. Leslie. Don thought he might be hiding something, but no idea what that could be. I guess there's no reason to think he's involved at all. The fact that Bobby spent time there, and it's so close to the casino makes me think we have to do some further exploration and that's happening as we speak."

For Marsh, there are no coincidences. I mainly agree with him but am not as strict an adherent to the axiom as he is.

He continued. "But at Fred's, we caught up with a bartender and a waitress at their favorite watering holes. Karin, the one who pointed you toward the Oceanview, was one. She didn't appear to know that she was setting you up. It surprised her because she kind of liked, or at least felt sorry for, Bobby. She was shocked to hear that he'd been killed and, with a little pressure about how her name might come up in the police investigation unless she could help us out, she told us what she knew about one Dorothy Mahoney, also known as Dot, aka Jane Morgan, aka Julie Kaminsky, aka Ruth Castro, aka Jewel Allen. That's what we've stumbled on so far. I'd guess there are more."

"Maybe she's into cosplay."

"Maybe. Or maybe she missed her true calling and should have headed for the bright lights of Broadway." Marsh paused and added, "Although I think she's not comfortable in the limelight, prefers to operate in the shadows."

"Her real name is Dorothy Mahoney?"

"Yes. Probably. That's what the California Department of Corrections thinks. We're still working on completing our background check."

Mahoney was a common name, so the feeling of recognition I got from it wasn't surprising. But it seemed to ring a too familiar bell in my recent memory I couldn't put a finger on right at that moment.

I shifted on the bed, rolled my legs out and over the side and planted them on the floor, moving my toes to get the circulation back. I winced and closed my eyes, feeling a sharp stab of pain in my temple. I rubbed the sleep out of my eyes with mild success.

"What else?" I mumbled.

"She's, more or less, an old-fashioned grifter. Served time for credit card and mail fraud of various sorts. She has a big heart. Enjoys working with old people. She cozies up to them, sometimes on the phone, sometimes just knocking on a lonely person's door, and then, after ingratiating herself, becomes best buddies. It isn't long before she's helping them with their finances, and not long after that, usually a matter of only days or weeks, that Grandma or Grandpa starts bleeding money."

"Bobby said she'd admitted to prison time but blamed it on a boyfriend who left her holding the dope."

"Any boyfriend of hers would have been the dope," Marsh said.

"So she probably had her eye on Bobby as a mark the whole time. Which was already obvious."

"Surely."

"I know what she looks like from her visit to *Acapella*. But a photo I can use to show around would help."

"The best one we have is the mug shot when she was arrested five years ago. She's stripped of makeup, her hair is kind of mousy, but there's something in her eyes and the curve of her mouth. Some men probably didn't mind being her dope."

"You'll get the photo?"

"Portia should be texting it in the next few minutes."

"But, and I assume you can corroborate this, from what Karin and the bartender said, she looks very different now. We showed them the mug picture, and they could hardly believe it was the same woman. She has brown hair, and I guess she's thinner and maybe has a new nose. Plus, the makeup adds a veneer of glamour. Course, she might have already shed that persona and look along with it. I would guess her look morphed along with her aliases."

"I think she toned it down while playing Bobby's daughter. Hair color is right, and she wasn't overly made up when she came to see me. I couldn't detect any plastic surgery, but maybe it was a good job. If I run into her, I'll know it."

"Unless she's already transforming herself into someone new. Especially with what went down at the motel, I would think..." He paused, and I listened to him thinking.

"We don't know that it was her and her gang that killed Bobby and Paula. It still seems likelier than Poe having anything to do with it. I think he had a soft spot for his brother. I can't imagine he'd murder him so ruthlessly. I know the trail's too fresh, but did you pick up any clues to where she's been spending her time since she left Bobby?"

"Karin didn't have any ideas about that. We tried to track her through two credit cards she uses under Jewel Allen but didn't come up with a lot. She hasn't used either card in more than a week."

"You said that you talked with a bartender. Was that a woman?"

"Yes. Maureen. She knew Jewel, but they weren't close."

"Did you talk to a woman named Selma?"

"Not in the notes here. We're still working our way through the employees. Some haven't taken shifts in the past day. Management is more than a little testy, so we're trying to catch people off duty, which takes time."

"Which we don't have," I muttered. "Any headway on the guys who were in her gang? The guys with her that day when Bobby overheard them?"

"Working on that. Karin mentioned a couple of guys who came in to see her fairly regularly, and she provided descriptions but no names. Once again, we checked at the gym and got no help from friend Leslie. Portia just got Bobby and Jewel's home phone call records and we're going through that identifying frequent callers. Time," he said.

"Which we don't have," I repeated. I had feeling this was all going to come to a head sooner rather than later, to say nothing of my involvement at the scene of the murders, which might stay hidden for one more day before I'd be on SFPD's most wanted list.

"The story just went up, boss." Someone talking to Marsh. The faint clicking of a keyboard. I waited.

"I'm reading about your adventures last night in the *Examiner*. Details are sketchy, thank goodness. Three bodies. Not identified. Horrific crime scene. Police not saying much. No mention of any names or suspects. Our friend in the department came through. Whoever committed the murders will wonder about the third body, whether it might be you. If they didn't mean to kill you, they'll wonder if they just hit you too hard. It'll make them have second thoughts, or think you are dead, and maybe allow us to catch them unawares."

"And you think later this morning they'll announce all of us poor victims' names?"

"That's the plan."

"I'm going to feel funny."

"Long as you don't feel dead."

"Still don't know why I'm not."

"That's what we'll find out, Plank." He paused, then added, "What's your day look like?"

"You're right about the bass. They're running."

"I can't join you today but have fun."

"I will. If I catch anything, I'll let you know."

"Ditto, partner."

TWENTY-ONE

Selma's eyes widened perceptibly as I approached the bar tucked into the shady back corner of Fred's Flapjack Casino.

As I placed my hands on top of the bar, she said, "The usual?"

I laughed, and she bent down and hoisted up a bottle of Ocean's Spray, filled a glass to the top with small rectangular ice cubes, filled it up with purple-red liquid, and dropped in a glistening twist of fresh lime.

She forgot my little paper umbrella, but I was still impressed.

She was wearing the same black dress and had the same perky breasts peeking above it. She also had the same glint in her eye. I felt liked, and that always brightens up a man's day.

I took a sip of cranberry and expressed my appreciation.

Selma said, "Didn't think I'd see you again so soon after Randy and Cro Magnon man attacked you yesterday."

I thought he was more akin to a Neanderthal, but at least we were on the same relative page. "Ah, I'm sure it was just a misunderstanding. They're both probably really nice guys who coach Little League on the weekends."

"Have you been drinking something other than cranberry?"

I laughed again. I liked her sense of humor. In another lifetime, I'd like to have spent more time with her.

"Randy isn't here this morning, but still, Max, he's got people spying on us. He'll know you were here and that you talked to me again."

I nodded. "I don't want to get you in trouble. But I wanted to ask you about Jewel Allen. She used to deal blackjack here."

She looked at me. Shook her head. "There's been too many people here lately asking about Bobby and Jewel. Randy's all paranoid about it. He told me specifically not to discuss her with anyone."

That was interesting. As much as I didn't want to spend more of time in the company of Randy, it might be unavoidable.

"When is your break?" I asked.

"Max," she said, sighing.

I flashed her an understanding but insistent smile.

WE SAT IN SELMA'S CAR, PARKED BENEATH THE SHADE OF A DYING elm tree bordering the casino, just beyond the chain-link fence enclosing a small parking lot for customers.

We were safely out of sight of the casino's potential prying eyes.

I'd left the casino almost forty minutes before she did and waited in a nearby Portuguese cafe, sipping black coffee and nibbling on a sweet roll.

Selma was puffing nervously on a cigarette. I tolerated it but had my window open. She told me about Jewel, rushing her words as if she had only a limited time. Her break was just fifteen minutes, and you had to punch in and out, and if you were late even five minutes, you got docked a half hour's pay.

Fred's Flapjack Casino was a blast from the past in more ways than one.

"I guess I wasn't level with you last time. I knew Bobby, mainly in terms of his relationship with Jewel, but I didn't know who you were really, and things have been paranoid there lately."

"But I thought you liked me."

"Yeah. Well, I've liked a lot of guys that screwed me."

"I can imagine."

She shook her head. "C' mon, I didn't mean that way."

"Sorry. I know what you meant. And there's no reason you should trust me, especially if Randy has been giving you such a hard time."

Two young boys on skateboards approached the car, jumping from the curb to the street. One of them, a shaggy redhead, slammed shoulder first into the car, his board skittering underneath. I moved to open the passenger door to check on him, but he bounced up with a laugh as his friend called him a moron, and he slithered under the car to retrieve the skateboard. A moment later, they disappeared around the corner. I thought of Frankie and her love and skill at skateboarding and realized I hadn't seen her for three days, that she was staying with Dao and Meiying thinking Alexandra and me were in Hawaii without her. I knew it made her sad and now it made me the same to think about it.

"Karin told me what happened to Bobby and his daughter. That's so horrible. That's why I'm here, despite Randy. I want to help if I can. I didn't know him well at all, but Bobby was nice. Naïve maybe. But not a mean bone in his body."

"What did you think of Jewel?"

"She was one of those women. Had a spark. Men loved her. She was pretty, sure, but she had something. And she knew what made men tick. Some women do and use it to help men out. Others, like Jewel, use it to their own advantage. Me, I've never been able to figure men out so much. I just like 'em."

"Nothing wrong with that."

"Well, it's gotten me into more trouble than it's worth sometimes."

I nodded.

"Anyway, Bobby was no match for Jewel. It was like a cat playing with a mouse. I don't know exactly what went on between them, but I wondered why she was with him at all. I knew he had to have something to offer her, but I never figured out what."

"Were you friends with her?"

"Not really. She didn't have a lot of time for other women. There were always men around her. She did go out with the girls a couple of times. I chatted with her about nothing special, but we weren't friends."

"Did you know she moved in with Bobby?"

"I heard."

"Do you have any idea where she might live now?"

"It's funny. It feels like, what do they call it, a deja vu moment. Is that right? Just this morning I saw her. And then you drop by unexpectedly asking about her. I guess there was a guy asking about her yesterday according to Karin, but it was my day off."

"You saw her this morning?" I said, feeling a surge of adrenaline.

"Yeah. I hadn't seen her in…I don't know. Weeks, I guess. And the last time I saw her, one night a while back, it was going in the gym too. I guess that isn't weird at all. Some guys I'd see her with were regulars at the gym."

"Do you know any of their names?"

"Who? The guys you mean?" She frowned, thinking. "I mean I didn't know them, but yeah, one was Carl, or maybe Carlos. That's it. Carlos. He was Latin. Kind of hunky in his own way. There was another guy name of Steve. I know they all spent time at the gym together. I don't know whether Jewel worked out.

That's a little hard to imagine. But the guys looked like weightlifters."

A crow landed on a power pole in my line of sight. He flapped his wings, and another crow dropped beside him. The second crow dug its beak into the middle of the first. There was a smattering of squawks and squeals and both of the birds lifted off, one chasing the other. Love or hate, I couldn't figure out which.

Another thing I couldn't figure out was why Jewel aka Paula had led me to investigate at Matthew's Maximizing Muscles if that was where she and her gang hung out. Had it all been a setup? Were Leslie and Carlos expecting me and directing me, however subtly, to the casino? Had Karin been in on it too?

Thinking back on the conversations I'd had with them all, I couldn't come to any conclusions as to why they thought I'd be a good patsy for them.

"Is Karin around today?" I asked.

"She's working the night shift. She should be here by nine tonight."

I couldn't wait for that.

"Do you know where she lives?"

Selma didn't want to tell me, but when I told her how important it was and offered a hundred-dollar bill in recompense for the half hour she'd be docked for coming back late for her break, she reluctantly relented.

"What time did you see Jewel?"

"It was early, before seven. I was having a smoke outside."

"Did she see you?"

"No, I don't think so."

I wrapped up with Selma quickly after that.

Jewel Allen had gone into the gym roughly two hours before.

If I was lucky, she was still there.

TWENTY-TWO

No surprise, the place looked exactly the same as it did the day before. A smelly, sweaty good old-fashioned place to build muscle. A manly enclave that I didn't imagine would be a natural place for Jewel Allen to hang out.

But then again, she seemed to have a way with men and was probably comfortable in their preferred haunts.

I, again, found Leslie at his desk. I got a surprised look from him, same as Selma had given me, but lacking any hint of her warmth or welcome.

Out in the gym behind us, there were a few guys pumping iron silently. Grunts proliferated. I didn't see Carlos. More importantly, I didn't see Jewel Allen. It wasn't a big place, but there was a back room behind the office that I assumed was used for storage and a bathroom that I guessed was gender neutral.

I, again, silently questioned Leslie's insistence that the gym was too full to take on the likes of me.

"I'm back," I said, cheerfully.

"Why?" he responded straight and to the point.

"I have a couple of questions."

"I told you everything I know about Bobby."

"I'm sure," I said. "Do you know a woman by the name of Jewel Allen?"

There was a long pause, and something flickered across his eyes. "No," he lied.

"I have it on reliable authority that she was here this very morning. A couple of hours ago. I don't think you could have missed her."

"I said I don't know her."

"Maybe she was using another name. She's known to do that. Can I describe her for you?"

"Ladies hardly ever come in here. There was no lady by any name here this morning. End of sentence. Period."

"Pardon, but I think you have that reversed. The saying goes: Period. End of sentence."

"You are an asshole."

I nodded. Fair assessment, from his point-of-view.

Leslie looked formidable. Lots of times with body builders, they appear tougher than they are. Their strength is all on the surface, in the muscle, but they don't have a clue as to how to use it effectively, and they're not quick or flexible. I had a feeling that this wasn't the case with Leslie. He was built like nobody's business, but he had a sleepy-eyed but tense quality to him, to the way he held himself, and unless I was wrong, he might present more of a challenge than the average man in his station.

After the blow to my head, I wasn't feeling tip top, and I had the impression that if I used force to try and convince Leslie of my seriousness, I might come out with even more damage that I could ill afford, even if I prevailed, which I expected to do.

While I studied him and contemplated the risk/reward ratio, I stepped around his desk and toward the back of the room. Leslie rose to stop me, but too late.

I was at the back-room door, turning the loose, tarnished

knob.

Leslie shouted, "What the hell do you think you're doing, asshole..." But he didn't have an interrogatory tone. As he charged toward me, I opened the door and stepped quickly around it, keeping my hand on the side jamb, waiting a precise moment, and then slamming it into Leslie's charging face.

He screamed, grabbed his nose, stumbled back. I stepped into his space and delivered one sharp jab with my right hand directly to his much-abused snout. I felt and then heard the crack of bone beneath my knuckles, confirming the break. Blood gushed from his face, and I danced away as Leslie collapsed backward on the ground, groaning and cursing in equal measure.

I went to the bathroom, found a roll of paper towels, wet and wadded up a bunch, and then brought it and the rest of the roll out. I knelt beside him, laid the wet clump over the hand that was clutching his face, and left the rest of the towels beside him.

I stood over him and waited for the cursing to stop. I felt bad although the punch, despite the pain that resulted in my hand, felt good. I had needed to hit something. I was feeling more ornery than usual as the result of the previous night's cataclysms and the throbbing pain in my noggin'. I didn't have much time, and Leslie was lying and wasting what precious little I had.

"Fucker, I'm going to have you arrested," he mumbled, stanching the flow of blood with the paper towels.

Not even a thank you for the first aid I'd provided.

"Get in line," I muttered back.

I left him there and returned to the back room, flipped on a light switch, and took its measure. It was a bigger-than-expected space, almost as big as the gym itself, and primarily a burial ground for retired exercise equipment: dumbbells, squat racks, kettlebells, bench presses, and more. Most of it was even more worn and damaged than the old stuff in the actual gym. The air was stale and full of dust. One corner contained a few boxes of office supplies: typing paper and its brethren, towels and Kleenex and TP.

I spotted another door at the south end of the room and marched toward it. I felt a rumbling of hooves behind me as I passed a nest of rusting kettlebells. I reached down and lifted one with a grunt, swinging it and me around into a crouching stance, cast iron weapon at the ready.

I counted three hulking behemoths clomping toward me.

I pounded the kettlebell three times hard against the concrete floor, feeling like the proverbial bull, wishing I could exhale hot steam through my nostrils to heighten the effect.

Still, it made my pursuers pause.

They stopped in their tracks and exchanged looks that were meant to reassure each other.

There are three of us, man, one of him. Kettlebell be damned.

What I had facing me was a trio of pseudo-alpha males. Even though one was black, one was Asian, and one white, they were all cut from the same mold. They'd all been inhabiting planet earth for roughly thirty years and were either bald or buzz cut, probably because it made them seem more intimidating. And they'd all spent too much time in gyms and too much money on steroids.

Just to show me that I wasn't the only one who could use handy tools, the Asian lifted what looked like a fifty-pound dumbbell and shook it at me, his eyes ablaze. That didn't bother me as much as the fact that he'd expended about as much effort as most people would in lofting a cupcake.

The other two followed suit, each of them handily snatching nearby heavy weights. On the plus side, I hadn't seen any guns yet.

Since I never believe that violence should be a first recourse, I called out to them. "Fellas, let's not do something we might regret later. I have a proposal," I said. I didn't but thought it might buy me a few seconds of time while I assessed.

That stopped them again and furrowed the brow of the

white guy.

I dropped the kettlebell, and it clanged to the floor, which made Asian guy flinch. I put my hands up, palms out, to show my innocent intention, and then used my words. "Really. What happened to Leslie was just an unfortunate accident. No harm meant. I even gave him the towels he's using on his nose. Honest. He told me it was okay to be back here as I'm looking for some-one. Maybe you guys know her? Jewel Allen. I think perhaps you're friends of hers. She's in a pickle and maybe we can work together to help her."

They watched me with semi-slack jaws, my reasoning, berserk as it was, serving to give them pause. Once again, they exchanged looks, perplexed this time, temporarily unsure about what I was saying and maybe even reconsidering whether violence was the answer.

I didn't really expect to convince them of anything. I was just hoping for a little more time.

"How do you know Jewel?" the bald black man said, doing a bicep curl with the dumbbell he'd lifted.

"Al, what the hell you doing?" White guy said. "He busted the boss's face open. He's after Jewel. He's trespassing. We gotta kick his ass."

"I know. I know, Earl. Just trying to figure out who this dude is before we kick his ass. Maybe he knows something. Something that can help us. Help Leslie and Jewel."

"Shut up, Al!" the Asian shouted. "You shouldn't be saying anything about anything in front of this guy. He could be a cop for all we know."

"Fucking right," Earl concurred.

"Jewel hired me," I said, "to help her out."

I was stating the God's honest truth.

"What the hell are you talking about?" Earl snarled.

"Just what I said. She thought I could help her find someone she needed to find. Guy by the name of Bobby."

"What the holy fuck!" Earl said, his face all scrunched up in what looked like horror.

I was on a roll and reaping a whole lot more grist for the mill than I'd ever expected from the responses of these intellectual titans.

"From what she told me, this guy had double crossed her and cheated her out of a lot of money. I've been looking for him, and I'm getting close, but I haven't been able to reach her for the past day, and I've got important information about where he might be hiding out." I was riffing like a crazy man now, inspired like Thelonious Monk improvising on a totally angular melodic twist.

And just like Monk, it made sense only in a hallucinatory way.

"Do you believe him, Earl?" Al asked, continuing to do bicep curls that I don't think he was even aware of.

Al looked at Earl as if the creature from *Alien* had just burst out of his chest. "How could you ask that question?"

Al's arm stopped the bicep curl in mid-motion and frowned. "I don't know. Just seems like we should be careful, in case Jewel needs this guy."

"In case Jewel needs this guy?" he said, and then, as if maybe he hadn't been heard, repeated it. "In case Jewel needs this guy? You have to be shitting me. I know you're kind of out-of-the-loop, Al, but I thought—" He stopped, shook his head. "Damn it. Nobody say nothing anymore. This guy's playing us. We've said too much. He's no friend of Jewel's or Leslie's. Fuck him. Let's take him out and let Leslie decide what to do with him."

At that moment, there was a knock at the back door.

The trio was just getting ready to charge me again. I held up my hand and said, "Wait just a minute, fellas. We have company."

They stared at me uncertainly.

Which was a mistake.

I walked to the door, unlocked it, and let Marsh in.

TWENTY-THREE

I no longer needed a kettlebell, which is just as well because somebody might have gotten hurt.

More than they actually got hurt.

Marsh insisted that I sit on the sidelines. I protested but not too much. I sat down on a cardboard box supposedly full of rubber mats. It sagged but didn't totally give way beneath my weight.

As Marsh turned to face them, the three fellas looked totally confused, their eyes moving from me, sitting passively out of the action, and this new guy, who really didn't look all that intimidating, ready to battle in my stead.

"What's going on here? Who the hell is this?" Earl asked.

To his credit, Marsh gave them a fair chance.

"Gentlemen, my associate and I have some questions for you. You are going to answer them honestly and to the best of your ability and then we'll be on our way. I would advise that you just sit down here," Marsh looked around, curled his lip up in an expression of distaste, and continued, "somewhere, and it should just take a few minutes of your time."

"You two are both out of your ever-fucking minds," Earl shouted.

"There may be some truth in that. But, I warn you, it will be a lot less painful if you answer our questions right now rather than after I mop up the floor with you."

Marsh glanced down, shook his head. "I've a mind to just mop up the floor with you anyway because it is disgusting. Why would the proprietor tolerate this?"

Earl and Al again looked at each other again, vexed, dismayed, and irritated.

I could have advised them that it's best not to let your emotions get carried away with you when dealing with Marsh. But I could tell it was already too late.

They charged. Led by Earl, with Al and nameless Asian right behind.

Marsh angled his left foot forward and waited. Earl came hurtling onward, ready to grab my friend in a headlock. Marsh let him close in, waited until Earl's hands were verily touching his shoulders before hooking his leg, his ankle, and simultaneously forking the tip of his fingers into his opponent's Adam's apple.

Earl's body twisted, jackknifed, as he grunted, grabbing his throat, gasping for breath. Marsh spun his body around and launched him into Al, and the two of them tumbled end over end with Al ending up on top of Earl, horrified, still trying to catch a breath.

The Asian, showing more agility and quickness than his comrades, dodged the falling bodies, dived to the ground, then attempted to launch himself upward at Marsh with a flashing knife that suddenly appeared in his hand.

Marsh grabbed his wrist and twisted, the knife clattered to the floor, and I heard a snapping sound as the Asian screamed. A moment later, he was on the ground with Marsh's foot on his throat, holding his wrist, writhing in pain.

Marsh left him there and ambled over to Al, who was trying to get out from under the struggling-for-breath, Earl. Marsh rolled Earl over and told him to relax and breathe through his nose. While holding his foot down on Al's solar plexus, he asked, "Do we have an understanding?"

Al nodded.

The whole thing was over in two blinks of an eye. It was like watching LeBron James dance and muscle his way through a slew of bulky defenders in the paint, before slamming a dunk shot through the hoop.

I PUT THE CLOSED SIGN ON THE GYM DOOR AND LOCKED IT AND returned to the supply room where the four wounded warriors sat up against the back wall, eyeing Marsh nervously.

Marsh had his hand loosely splayed on a small revolver lying on the box he was sitting on while he hummed a variation of "To Dream the Impossible Dream" from *Man of La Mancha*.

I sat down beside him on a matching cardboard box and looked at the motley crew in front of me.

Leslie had his eyes fixed on me, while his left hand held the wad of wet towels against his nose. They were stained to a reddish black color, but it appeared that he'd stemmed the flow of new blood.

Earl, breathing a tad more freely now, stared humbly down at his cowboy boots. Al was looking at Marsh with awe in his eyes. The Asian guy was shaking his head back and forth, holding his wrist with a woe-is-me expression on his face.

"Fellas," I began, "sorry it had to come to this, but we don't have much time here. I have a few questions for you, and, if I think you've been honest in your answers, we can all proceed on to the tasks of the day. Is that acceptable to you all?"

None of them bothered with even a grunt of assent. Nevertheless, I persisted.

"First of all, a three-part question. I want you to tell me what Jewel Allen was doing here earlier today and what your involvement with her is and has been. And the bonus question of the day, for five hundred dollars and a chance at Final Jeopardy, where has she gone to from here?"

None of them laughed or rushed to answer me.

I decided to go for broke. After all, I was going to be named any time now in the local media as having died at the Beachside Motel with Bobby and Paula. We'd hoped to fool the killers, to stir up action, to buy time, but if the men in front of me were responsible for the deaths, then none of that mattered as they obviously were aware I was still breathing. None of them, excepting Leslie, seemed to recognize me, so I didn't think we'd found our killers quite yet.

"Leslie," I said. "C'mon, man. you're going to talk to me or the police. Your guys here have already let the cat out the bag. They know Jewel. They were probably accomplices with her in what went down at Pirate's Cove. Maybe they murdered Bobby and Paula. I can go to the police, or, even worse, tell Poe that all of you were involved in killing his brother."

Leslie looked at me for a long time with an expression in his eyes of utter contempt. I understood. I'd humiliated him, and he'd had enough of that growing up. I didn't feel good about it.

Finally, he turned to the others and said, "What the hell did you tell this jerk?"

Al mumbled, "Nothing, boss."

Earl muttered, "Al believed this guy's BS. He was telling us that he was helping Jewel. That she hired him to find Bobby. Al let on that we knew her. I told him to shut up but—"

"Christ," Leslie groaned, closing his eyes. He dropped the paper towels from his face and opened his eyes. His nose was swollen and bent at a slightly different angle than before and there was dried blood encrusted beneath his left nostril.

Just then Marsh's phone rang, and he said, "Excuse me, gentlemen." He got up and walked away to take the call.

"Leslie, I'm beginning to think that you and Jewel were associates. That you had something to do with the scams at Pirate's Cove and maybe even the killings of Bobby and his daughter. Maybe somebody panicked. You were afraid that Bobby was going to go to the cops or, even worse, Poe. You went a little crazy and killed them and somehow thought you could pin it on me, and that's really…"

Marsh sat back down next to me, leaned in, and whispered the news of the day into my ear. That stopped me in my tracks, and I pulled back and looked at Marsh. "Really?" I said.

He nodded. I looked back at Leslie, studying him.

"Marsh," I said, "can you finish up with our friends here? I don't care what you have to do, just make sure that they come clean about everything they know. If you think they're lying, employ whatever you used at Guantanamo until they're begging you to fess up."

"Okey-dokey. Sounds like fun," Marsh replied, clapping his hands with relish.

I gave the trio the evil eye. I didn't know if Marsh had ever been to Guantanamo Bay during his occasional secret forays. The point was to put the fear of God in the minds of Earl and Al.

"This is all bullshit. Don't tell him a thing," Leslie barked to the men.

Marsh twirled his revolver by the handle like a gunslinger and slid it smoothly back into a case inside his jacket. He reached down and lifted his pants leg and removed a very intimidating looking knife with a hooked blade. It was a Kukri, an ancient weapon employed by the elite Nepalese Brigade of Gurkhas. A multi-use instrument perfect for simultaneously slicing and chopping.

Marsh held it up to a fluorescent overhead bulb and examined it nonchalantly. Beads of sweat broke out on Al's forehead.

"Leslie," I said, "let's leave my friend to his work. You and me need to talk. Back to your office."

"What the hell is this now?" Leslie answered, before looking into my eyes. He took in what was there, sighed, struggled to his feet, and followed me out.

TWENTY-FOUR

I closed the door to the supply room and motioned for Leslie to sit back in his office chair. I stood with my back to the door and waited until he was settled. He was a none-too-happy man, and it wasn't just about his nose.

"Your partner, Matthew, his last name was Mahoney, right?"

Leslie looked at me but didn't answer.

"Jewel Allen's real name is Dorothy Mahoney. Matthew had a daughter by that name, and they are one and the same person."

Portia, Poe's crack computer hacker, had managed to make the connection.

"So what?" Leslie sneered.

"It's over. Either talk to me or I call the cops right now and tell them that you not only were involved in the casino cheat but that you had something to do with the murders. Your friends back there are going to tell us everything they know. You know they are. Marsh isn't going to even have to break a sweat."

Leslie tried to hold my accusatory stare, tried to stay tough, but his eyes filled with tears, and he closed them with a shudder that racked his body. He grabbed his arms with his hands and leaned forward. Blood began trickling out of his broken nose again and dropping onto the floor. He gasped, put his fingers up, and wiped it away. He put his hands on his knees, steadied himself, and said, "It was all Jewel's, Dot's, idea. She was always working some angle, always looking for the big score. She drove her father crazy, but he wouldn't give up on her. He blamed himself for the way she was. But if you ask me, she was born that way. Nothing he could ever do about it."

He stopped, pinched his nose lightly, regaining his composure. He sat up straight and rolled his shoulders back as if better posture would fix everything.

I just waited, letting him recover.

"Why did he blame himself?"

"He left the girl's mother, and she killed herself a year later. That was when Dot was eleven. He raised her by himself from there, did everything he could to give her a normal life, but he always took responsibility for his ex-wife's death and the bad effect it had on Dot."

I nodded, and he added, "I should never have told her how pissed I was at Poe."

"What do you mean?"

"He owns this building. It's not in his name, of course. I think he owns most of half the real estate on this block. Through different dummy corporations or various trusts that he controls. Not Fred's across the street, but he keeps offering to buy them out. Fred never will. He hates Poe. Randy, his son, is a different story. He'd sell his balls for the right price."

"What does that have to do with anything?" I asked, although the bigger picture was starting to clarify just a little. I thought about Poe and his tentacles spread far beyond his casino enclave on Treasure Island, influencing and infecting unknown parts of the Bay Area and beyond.

"Just before Matthew died, about a year ago, the lease came up for renewal and Poe tripled the rent. It near drove Matthew crazy. He loved this place. It was his life's work. The two of us have run it together for the past twenty two years. Matthew had stomach cancer, and I think dealing with Poe shortened his life. He was distraught about it, afraid he'd lose the place. Poe wouldn't give an inch. Said he had tenants begging him for the place. I didn't believe him, but what could we do? We've been struggling, running big losses every month. I got an inheritance from my mom when she died a few years ago, but it's almost gone. I was out of ideas."

He paused, got up, walked to a water cooler next to the bathroom, filled a paper cup, and sipped it down. He returned to his chair, sagged wearily back down into it.

"Dot came back into town about six months ago. She'd been in prison and God knows where else after she got out. Said she'd spent time in New York." He sighed, shook his head. "You couldn't trust anything she said. Anyway, one night I was so frustrated after paying Poe his monthly ransom that I mentioned it to Dot and how I'd promised her father on his deathbed that I'd protect the place. That I'd never let Poe close us down.

"The next day she comes to me with this cockamamie scheme of hers. Tells me she knows a lot about gaming and casinos and that she knows guys who can help her and me get money from Poe's casino. She tells me how important her father's legacy is to her too. I doubted her, but I was out of options. She can be very convincing, and I was so angry with Poe and well...I owed it to Matthew. I loved him. He was the love of my life." He closed his eyes again, and his shoulders began spasming as tears rolled down his cheeks.

Staring at the floor, he said, "Matthew left his wife for me. And Dot knew it. Both of us always carried a load of guilt about that."

I took a deep breath and blew it out through my mouth, trying to absorb and make sense of what this new information meant for the whole rotten affair, the scams and the murders, and if the same perps were behind both.

As usual in human relations and evil doing, everything was much more complicated than it seemed. "So Al and Earl and friend back there were all involved in the scams?"

"Only Earl. The other two don't know much. I don't even know all of it. Carlos, I think you met him when you were here, was involved. His specialty is blackjack. There were five others, and they've all been hanging out here on and off for the past few months. Carlos was kind of a co-conspirator with Jewel. He had her ear like no one else."

I wouldn't have guessed that from our conversation about Bobby, but it had been brief, and I'd had no reason to doubt him at the time.

"What did they need you for?"

"Money. I gave them the rest of my mother's inheritance to front them the cash they needed to gamble as well as pay for some electronic equipment used to manipulate the roulette ball."

"And you were supposed to split the proceeds with Dot and these men?"

"Half to me and the other half was up to Dot to divide up. They pinched Poe for more than a million bucks is my understanding. But I haven't seen a dime of it. Dot kept telling me it was coming. That's what she told me this morning when she was here. Only a couple more days. I'm already late on this month's rent. I don't know why I trusted her. I knew better, but I was just so overwhelmed. I couldn't disappoint Matthew. If I lost this gym...I don't know, after he died, I'd have no reason to keep living."

If I had to bet on it, I'd wager that Leslie was telling me mostly the truth. His words were raw, and his emotions seemed real.

I was listening with one ear cocked toward the supply room. I hadn't heard any screaming so, as I expected, Marsh hadn't had to resort to pain to have his way.

"So you and Dot decided at some point that Bobby and his daughter were too big a risk. Did you think that out or did something go wrong and somebody panic?"

"No," he said, with a bite. "I don't know anything about that. Dot told me this morning that somebody had murdered them. It was the first I'd heard of it." He reached up and touched his raw nose, wiped sweat off his brow. "Jeez. I was stunned. I don't know if she was involved. She denied it. She said she'd only found out through a source that she couldn't tell me about because it was too dangerous. I don't know what to believe."

"Were you there the night that Bobby was up in his loft and overheard Jewel and her gang? When they threatened him?"

"I don't know what you're talking about."

I assumed from what Leslie said that Earl was one of the men involved that night along with Carlos. I'd check Leslie's story against his.

Leslie seemed to be leveling with me completely now, but I knew I couldn't trust him. It was one thing to admit to being involved in a casino scam and quite another to admit that you were a murderer.

I asked a few more questions and got the names of the other two men involved with Jewel and then rose to join Marsh in the stock room.

"What are you going to do?" Leslie asked as I was leaving.

"I don't know."

"Are you going to the police?"

"Not right now."

We exchanged a long, sad look before his eyes turned away.

I left him there, broken nose and all.

TWENTY-FIVE

"**D**o you believe him?" Marsh asked.

We were sitting in his Tesla, a block south of Matthew's gym.

"Mostly."

"You don't think he had anything to do with the murders?"

"I don't know. Maybe not. Maybe it was just Jewel who set it up. According to most everyone who knew her, she was without scruple. Although she's never been accused of anything violent. It's always been grifts."

"We don't know that. She'd probably have a man do her dirty work for her."

"True. And she has to be our most likely candidate." I was watching the street. A man teetering on his heels and holding a paper bag in his hand smoked a cigarette while leaning back against a utility pole. A black cat licked its paws beside a patch of dead grass in front of a hardware supply business. Other than that, it was pretty deserted. I wondered how Matthew and Leslie and Fred had kept their ventures going for the past twenty years with such an off-the-beaten-path location, more suited for industrial uses than retail.

I guessed it was akin to the out-of-the-way great breakfast place that draws a crowd. Leslie and Fred offered a unique experience, out of step with the au courant style, but popular enough for a cult following.

"Is Alexandra in place?" Marsh asked.

"Yeah."

"You going to join her?"

"Tonight."

"You okay with that?"

"I know she can take care of herself, but it worries me, of course."

He nodded and said, "What now, then?"

"We've got to find Jewel. Our friends back there have any idea where she might be?"

"Earl said he thought she'd been living at a different motel every night lately, from what she'd hinted. But he wasn't even sure of that. He said she'd gotten paranoid lately and didn't trust anybody. She wouldn't say what was going on, but indicated that she was working on something big. Which Earl said wasn't unusual for her, but this time, she was more on edge. When she showed up at the gym this morning, it was a surprise to everybody. She met with Leslie in his office for a few minutes and then left without talking to anyone else."

"I guess I should start with Carlos. Leslie got me his home and work addresses. He said that he usually comes in the gym late afternoon, but we can't wait that long. Could you check out the others—Pency, Jorge, and Julian—who Leslie claims were actually involved in the scams at Pirate's Cove?"

Marsh took the information, and without further ado, we agreed to check back in with each other as soon as there was anything worth sharing.

I wouldn't have pegged Carlos for a florist.

Weightlifting and petunias aren't usually associated. Florists and blackjack sharks don't seem to go together.

I wondered how many florists were also killers.

He owned a nursery, Calla Lilies & More, in South San Francisco, near Cypress Lawn Cemetery where my father was buried. As I passed the sprawling, rolling lawns, I realized it had been years since I'd bothered to visit his crypt.

Dad and I had had more than our share of difficulties, but he'd done the best he could. I don't live in the past and hardly ever dwell on it, but I owed him a visit.

Mom wasn't too far away, in a nursing home in Colma. She's suffered a few strokes and has dementia. Sometimes she recognizes me, sometimes not. I normally visit her every couple of weeks. It had been close to a month now, and I promised myself that as soon as this case was wrapped up, I'd go see her and hope it was one of her better days.

She'd been a good mom, mostly, although she didn't really understand me. Course, I can't think of a single woman who ever has.

That's not really true though, if I think about it. The exception is staring me right in the face if I just acknowledge it.

Anyway, Mom was an angel who sacrificed herself for her husband and me and my sister without getting much in return.

It was kind of a cemetery row down on the peninsula with a dozen or more of them lined up off State Route 82, the El Camino Real—the King's Highway linking the twenty-one California Spanish missions—running from Daly City to San Mateo.

So Calla Lilies & More was well located to take advantage, and Carlos seemed to be doing exactly that.

The place was mobbed with patrons. It was a small store made largely of glass, stuffed to the gill with flowers and plants. Three golden bells dangling from red and green ribbons announced my arrival, and I was greeted with the strong scent of a hundred different blossoms. Or so it seemed. The leaves of blooming plants hanging above brushed my hair as I moved through the rainbow-colored space.

Two young females were behind a desk preparing flowers and plants, nipping buds, wrapping roses in cellophane, chattering with customers about how lovely it all was.

I spotted Carlos beside a refrigerated display case, holding a bouquet of roses up for inspection by an elderly woman with shellacked silver hair.

He was wearing khaki shorts and a short-sleeve shirt, and his biceps bulged as he waved a rose to and fro. The woman's eyes tried valiantly to stay on the lovely red flower but kept straying to Carlos's even more fascinating musculature.

I walked over and hovered behind the woman who was wearing a flowing pink caftan and had a pink and yellow daisy sticking incongruously out of a tie in her hair. I couldn't decide if she'd put it there, or it had fallen from above and stuck to the thick layer of sticky stuff holding her hair pressed down to her skull.

Despite the fact that I towered over the petite lady, Carlos didn't seem to notice me as he continued gesticulating and flexing, telling the woman all about the history and appropriateness of this particular set of roses for her purposes.

Finally, I interrupted. "Carlos."

He looked startled, shook his head, found me. "What?" he said.

"Remember me? From the gym. We talked about Bobby."

The smile he'd been flashing vanished.

The little lady turned her face to me for a moment, frowning, bothered about the rude interruption.

"I'm busy right now," Carlos said.

"We need to talk."

"I'm sorry. Not during store hours."

"It's urgent," I said.

"We close at three today. Perhaps then."

"That won't do," I said.

"Excuse me for a moment, Mrs. Richards. I'll be right back."

He took my elbow and steered me to a little alcove festooned with balloons and ribbons beside the refrigerated case. "What do you want?" he asked.

"I want to know about Jewel Allen."

His eyelids fluttered, lowering for a moment, as if he was trying to shut something down. "I don't know anything about her. And, as I said, now's not the time. I'm a busy man. Look at all this." He waved, pointing out the obvious popularity of his busy little fiefdom. "Now I must go," he said, and returned to Mrs. Richards who was studying us, or more specifically, him, with an eager eye.

After apologizing for me, he launched back into his spiel, and she listened, enraptured. I watched them for a few seconds, feeling what I felt.

I moved away and found a spot in a corner of the store where the floor was covered with a jungle of potted flowers. I planted myself amongst them and peered down into the mass of semi-natural life.

I drew a deep breath, let it go, and shouted, "Oh my god, a snake! Jeez, how'd a rattler get in here! Everybody run!"

And I galloped out of the store.

TWENTY-SIX

A general uproar and pandemonium followed my departure.

Even Carlos's two employees deserted, shrieking all the way.

I threaded back through the crowd now gathered outside discussing the dreaded rattler as if it were Voldemort's evil snake come to life. I reassured one and all, telling them that animal control was on the way and that I was going to check on poor Carlos inside, warning them to come no closer.

I found the florist sitting on a stool inside his now empty store.

"Are you out of your mind?" he said, shaking his head like he was in the presence of true insanity.

I'd been accused of that more today than usual, and it made me wonder for just a moment before I realized that it was my job, not me, that was crazy.

"I warned you it was urgent."

"Do you know what this can do to my business? I'm going to—"

"Shut up!" I shouted. "You're in deep shit, friend. Leslie told me you were involved in cheating the Pirate's Cove Casino among other prosecutable offenses."

His eyes danced around the room, then veered to the window looking out at the throng of would-be customers. "What do you want?"

"Like I said, I'm looking for Jewel Allen."

"I can't help you."

"Can't or won't?"

"Can't. I don't know where she is."

"Tell me what you know about her. You were her blackjack guy, right?"

"I have no idea what you're talking about. I'm a florist."

I studied him, trying to decide on my best tack. "You were friends with Bobby. Or that's what you told me."

He gripped his knees with his hands. "We weren't close friends, but yes, we worked out together, shared a few breakfasts. He cried on my shoulder. I tried to help him out."

"Were you there at Bobby and Jewel's place the night he over-heard her and found out how she was using him, betraying him just for access to information about his brother's casino?"

Carlos gave me a cold stare, nothing more.

"When was the last time you talked to Bobby?"

"I don't know. I guess the last time he was at the gym. A week ago, maybe, perhaps longer."

"And that was the last time you saw him?"

"That's what I said."

"What did he seem like? What was his mood?"

"I don't know. Same as ever. He was a nervous guy."

He was a decent liar. He didn't seem shocked at all at the mention of Bobby. If he knew about the murders, he was acting like he didn't.

This was all bullshit. I glanced behind me, surveying the

crowd. No one was making a move to re-enter. I knew I didn't have much time. I thought about planting Carlos's head in a planter until he started telling the truth, but it would be hard to hide the commotion from the lookie-loos and, since I was supposed to be dead, I didn't want any calls to or intervention from the police.

"You're lying to me. You're in trouble. I don't know what your story is. Why someone with a successful business like this would be involved in a casino cheat. I don't care at this point. I'll let the cops sort that out with you. And that's the least of your worries. Soon, Poe's going to find out you were stealing his money, and then you're going to be knee deep in it."

He shrugged.

"Has Jewel handed over your share of the take yet?"

He gave me a blank stare.

"Leslie tells me she stiffed him so far."

He stayed tight as a drum.

I needed more time with him. I needed to get him alone.

"You don't have any idea where Jewel is now?"

He rolled his eyes dismissively.

"This is your last chance. It's all coming down, and it's going to bury you. I'd say this is the last day in the flower business for you. Give me a little help, a nudge in the right direction, and I'll remember it. I'll do what I can when the time comes. With the police and with Poe. I have a little influence in both quarters."

Carlos laughed, but his eyes didn't look amused. "Yeah. I trust you."

"You can trust me a whole hell of a lot more than you can trust Jewel Allen. She's double crossed just about everybody she's ever been involved with."

"She'll never double cross me," he said. "She loves—" He stopped, swore. "Get the hell out of my store," he muttered.

"You're a fool. Watch your back, Carlos. They're coming for you."

I left him there, opened the shop door, the little bells merrily signaling my departure, and waded into the anticipatory faces of the crowd of former customers.

"My mistake," I called out. "It was just a garter snake. Big one though. I was sure I heard it rattling, but Carlos says its harmless."

I left them there, nervously eyeing the formerly heart-warming, but now fraught-with-peril, shop.

TWENTY-SEVEN

Carlos kept turning around every few seconds, surveying the landscape behind him, as if he knew that I was following.

I was sure he hadn't spotted me. I stayed roughly fifty yards behind him, favoring shadows cast by the morning sun, the entries of various death-related enterprises, and the trunks of Cypress and Eucalyptus trees.

I'd shaken his tree, and he was responding as I'd hoped.

He gave a little speech to the customers waiting anxiously outside—I couldn't hear his words from my vantage point inside the shop of a headstone dealer across the street, but it was obvious that he was reassuring them about the snake and perhaps claiming that I was either a nut case or a hysteric.

He waved at them with a big smile, and the customers, one after the other, turned and slowly wandered away.

He re-entered the shop alone, and I could see him bustling about inside. He spent a couple of minutes talking on his cell phone, gesticulating to beat the band.

I waited, fending off a salesman trying to interest me in the elaborate marble headstone fit for an Egyptian Pharaoh that I was standing beside.

After around ten minutes, Carlos flipped the sign on the shop door from open to closed and stepped outside where he locked up and hurried away on foot.

I knew that he lived less than a mile from the shop and figured he either walked or cycled back and forth.

HE WAS HEADING SOUTH, TOWARD HIS HOUSE ON E STREET IN Colma, opposite the Italian and Japanese cemeteries. Carlos was surrounded personally and professionally by dead bodies, and I wondered if that had finally gotten to him.

My cell phone vibrated in my front pants pocket, and I let it go, taking cover within the curlicued arches made of faux granite marking the entry to a funeral home. The shadows cast by two towering elms served to conceal me. I let Carlos move farther away from me now that I was sure he was headed home.

I slid out my cell phone and glanced at the screen where I found the shockingly off-putting message:

You're Dead!

Attached was a link that I clicked on taking me to the website of the *San Francisco Examiner*. The story there gave more details about the murders the previous night at the Beachside Motel, most relevant of which were the names of the three victims: Bobby Fenderdale and his daughter, along with the name of a local private investigator of a sort, Max Plank. The only other thing mentioned was that I lived on a boat at Fisherman's Wharf. That fact was added, I'm sure, because the reporter knew that the lifestyle fascinates people. The romantic life of a now dead P.I.

You might have envied him, but look, he's dead now.

I must say that reading about your own death has a bracing effect. I looked forward to the obituary, if it came to that, wondering if they'd dig up any tasty morsels of biography that I'd tried to bury.

I typed in a quick response to Marsh—"Better dead than sorry"—and put the phone back.

Carlos was out of sight now, so I walked out onto the bright sunlit curb and, pacing myself so I wouldn't catch him before he neared home, took my daily dose of vitamin D from the half-blazing rays.

I CAUGHT UP WITH HIM AS HE TURNED FROM THE EL CAMINO REAL onto E Street.

I darted up F Street, to the south of his home block, and trotted up past a park and recreation center, a tennis court, and then a large apartment building. I rounded the corner at Clark Street, hurrying until I reached his tree-lined house on the corner of E and Clark.

It was surrounded by a white picket fence enclosing intricately patterned flower beds featuring Greek statuary—toga-clad maidens posing with wine jugs and a fountain with burbling water.

Beside the fence was a white door with a knocker that looked like the front door to the house leading into the first-floor level.

I glanced around the corner and spotted him half a block away. I backed up and sheltered myself behind a giant Eucalyptus tree that bordered one side of his house beside a stairway that rose to its second level.

A few seconds later, Carlos used that staircase, rather than the front door, to enter his house.

I waited until he was safely inside and then followed in his footsteps.

TWENTY-EIGHT

The door was hidden from the street by the trees, so I put my ear to its scarred wood surface without worrying about what the neighbors might be thinking.

As I strained to hear any little telling sounds, John Malkovich's sing-song voice from the *Saturday Night Live* skit where he's scaring the hell out of a group of innocent children—*not a creature was stirring, not even a mouse*—ran through my mind.

Perhaps the knock on the head had taken its toll.

I shook off the notion and John Malkovich.

But I hadn't heard a thing.

I stepped back and studied the porch, a stoop really, and the door itself and contrasted that to the first-floor entry, considering my options.

The first floor was open to the street, and though all was deserted at the moment, the view was visible from several nearby windows and any passersby who might suddenly appear.

Whatever I decided to do up here on the porch would go unnoticed save for the cardinal currently looking up at me from its perch on the shoulders of the stone cold Greek lovely caressing the jug at the bottom of the stairs.

I thought about just charging the door using my body as a battering ram. It didn't look all that strong. But the stoop didn't provide room for me to build up any kind of momentum, and unless I busted it off its hinges in one fell swoop, it would completely foil any attempt at a surprise entrance.

I trotted gingerly back down the stairs and, watching my surroundings, tried my luck at the two windows I'd spotted earlier in the back yard.

Locked, as I'd expected.

I glanced over at the front door and quickly surmised that it looked sturdier, presenting a bigger challenge that its upstairs sister.

I watched the cardinal watch me for a few seconds before it got bored and took flight. I realized I was just avoiding the only viable option and that maybe my mind was still disordered from last night's hit.

But then, suddenly, I was struck by a thought, an aha moment.

I returned to the stairs and climbed half-way up before stopping. I fished my cell phone out of my pocket and retrieved the business card where I'd recorded the information that Leslie had given me.

Then I tapped in the number that I found there.

IT ONLY TOOK CARLOS AROUND FIFTEEN SECONDS TO OPEN THE porch door and scramble down the stairs.

As I expected, he cared deeply about his Greek maidens and was distraught to hear a stranger telling him that someone was in his yard with a baseball bat smashing them to pieces.

I tripped him as he rounded the corner, and he landed face

first into the low-maintenance white gravel. At that moment, he probably wished he'd planted grass instead.

He grunted, whined, screamed, but I was on him, my hand muffling the sound bursting from his battered lips. I grabbed him from behind, holding his belt and shirt, and jerked him to his feet.

He was a mess, his mouth full of gravel, his forehead and cheeks and chin cut and bleeding. He looked at me with crazy eyes and tried to swing at my face, but I spun him around and then march-stepped him back toward the stairs. He stumbled forward, trying to resist, so I stomped on his heel and kicked him in the ass, and he groaned again and started to shout. I reached around, slapped him hard on the side of the face, and snarled in his ear to shut up or I'd kill him, or something like that.

He whined and cursed, but with less volume and gusto, and I pushed him to the stairs and forced him up with my knee between his legs, threatening more damage.

When we reached the porch, I steered him through the open door and then pushed him hard, and he stumbled and fell onto the black ceramic tile entryway. He grunted, rolled over, looked up at me, and covered his bloody mess of a face with the palms of his quivering hands.

"Now," I said, "we're going to get—"

And for the second time in as many days, my head exploded, the lights went out, and I was lost to the world.

TWENTY-NINE

I came to with an all-of-a-sudden start, a jerk of my head.
My eyes flashed open.
My mind was remarkably clear, as was my vision.

But it hurt. It really hurt. The pain behind my eyes was astronomical. If I had the choice of getting rid of that pain or dealing with the everlasting fires of hell itself, at that moment, I would have chosen the latter.

I closed my eyes and tried not to gasp or burst into tears. I made no sound but felt drops of the liquid stuff running down my cheeks.

I gritted my teeth, opened my eyes, and grimaced, whimpering while looking around.

I was lying on a white bearskin rug in front of a Swedish fireplace in the middle of a room that looked like a hunting lodge. I vaguely registered mounted birds and rodents or mammals of the high desert along with a couple of big cat heads on the wall.

Carlos was full of surprises and contradictions. With every new bit of information, I liked him less.

I tried to get my bearings, to think about what had happened, who had hit me. I tried not to think about how damn stupid I'd been.

Suddenly I remembered arming myself from the hidden compartment in *Acapella Blues*. My hands scrambled for the gun inside my coat.

The holster was empty.

I groaned and reached down to feel for the knife strapped to my shin and found that I'd been stripped of that too.

"Plank, you're an idiot," I whispered, biting my lip from the pain in my head.

My thoughts were even more slanderous of my character.

Despite feeling that if I moved a muscle, the pain might render me unconscious again, I managed to prop myself up on my elbows.

I heard muted voices coming from somewhere nearby. At least two people, maybe more. And one of them was a woman.

I closed my eyes and tried to think.

Was Jewel Allen here?

God, I wanted to meet that woman, but, I thought, the current circumstances were just a tad short of ideal.

Carlos had let slip that he trusted her, that they had a close relationship. He'd actually almost said that she loved him, hadn't he?

So her presence here shouldn't have been surprising.

Should it, Plank?

Idiot.

I patted my front pants pocket and, as expected, found myself phoneless.

No means of protection or communication so I'd have to use my wits.

Big trouble.

If these were the murderers—and if they weren't, none of this made much sense—I could see no reason why they wouldn't continue their spree. They were probably discussing the best way to dispose of my body right now.

At that moment, I would have sold my soul for a full bottle of Oxycontin. I wanted to curl up into a ball and die. I wanted to cry out for my mommy.

Instead, I struggled up into a sitting position, and slowly, slowly turned my head on its unsteady axis to study the room for an escape route.

I was on the first floor in a weird facsimile of a hunting lodge, which was just a large converted bedroom that someone had centered with the Swedish fireplace, painted red, and run a flue up, impractically and expensively, two stories.

Which meant that they'd dragged me downstairs after knocking me out. I pictured Carlos, in an angry revengeful mood, dragging me down the stairs by my legs, my head bouncing hard against each wooden step.

I noticed a single closed door that I assumed led into the main part of the house. That was where the voices were coming from.

There were three. Two men and one woman. The two men were agitated; the woman seemed calm, cool, collected.

This worried me.

I preferred adversaries that were in a state of panic.

On the side opposite the door were two windows covered with blinds, each of which were four-paned, several feet off the ground.

I got up on my hands and knees, my teeth hurting from the grinding I was giving them. With a muted grunt, I lifted myself up and onto a decidedly unsteady footing.

I had no idea how long I'd been out, but I didn't think it had been more than a few minutes. The light streaming in from the blinds was bright, and it just felt like not much time had passed. Perhaps that's why I had been left alone for a while because they didn't expect me to recover so soon.

Was there any reason for them to keep me alive?

I couldn't think of one. Not after Carlos told Jewel about my line of questioning.

Even though my death wouldn't solve all their problems, they still had Poe to deal with. And Marsh. They didn't realize what kind of wrath he would unleash if they harmed me. Killing Bobby and Paula proved how foolish and impulsive they were.

I couldn't rely on logic or mercy.

There was never enough logic or mercy in this fallen world of ours, but I decided not to spend time mourning that fact right then and there.

The door to the room suddenly burst open, and Carlos appeared with a gun in his hand.

It wasn't mine, but that gave me no comfort.

Behind him, I glimpsed the shadow of a female form.

He shouted at me, "What the hell?" He raised the gun and ordered, "Don't move a muscle."

My body pleaded with me to obey him. It really did.

It wanted the bullet to end my pain.

I turned back toward the window, hesitated not even a moment, and charged it with all my limbs wind-milling like the completely crazy man that I felt like.

Just before I hit the window, I lowered my shoulder and felt something whir and whistle by my face.

A half-moment later, I burst through, shards of glass and splintered wood exploding in the air around me, as I tumbled and arced my body, end over end, attempting to land on the gravel outside with my ass.

I landed on my side, feeling a rip and burn in my left shoulder, but I'd found temporary relief from pain via the adrenaline pumping through my veins.

I lay there for a moment, dazed, without a thought.

Carlos appeared at the window, again leveling the gun toward me. I scrambled in the gravel, twisting my body this way and that, feeling pathetic and hapless.

"Hey, Mr. C," a young boy cried out from his bike across the street. "Who's that guy in your yard?"

That gave Carlos pause.

And me an opening.

Using one of the Greek stone maidens for support, I scrambled to my feet, glancing back to find Carlos, his blood-streaked face a mass of anger and frustration, his eyes jumping from me to the young boy, his gun out of sight now.

Behind him was a woman whose face was half-hidden in shadow.

I turned and ran clumsily, lopsidedly, out of the yard and down E Street, shuffling like a madman.

THIRTY

Now that pay phones have gone the way of DVD players and dinosaurs, I had a hard time scaring up a call.

Or, more accurately, I scared everybody I approached who was using a cell phone on the street. I couldn't really blame them. I must have looked a fright, and my words were a jumble of confusion.

Two women hurried away before I could even complete a sentence, and a man in a business suit just shook his head and went back to his texting. Normally, I would have just snatched the phone out of his hand, but I didn't have the energy.

Finally, I prevailed upon a young boy, probably only eight or nine, who was hanging out near the Colma Bart station a few blocks from Carlos's house. The kid was playing *Fortnite* on his phone, and I convinced him with the benefit of a ten-dollar bill I found in my jacket pocket. I had no idea how it had gotten there, but was thankful to the Gods for small favors.

I made the call, handed over the ransom, and the kid went back to his game.

I sat down on a bench outside the station and waited, trying to stay alert, my eyes combing the surroundings for any sign of Carlos or Jewel or other shady characters. I didn't figure they'd follow me. I assumed they wouldn't attempt to kill me out on the streets in broad daylight.

They were probably gone. On the run.

But where would they go?

Maybe Jewel was in love with Carlos and the two of them were going to escape to Borneo or Bali with all that loot and live happily ever after.

I waited no more than fifteen minutes until a long black limousine with shaded windows pulled up in front of my bench.

The driver, a Samoan man in a tight black t-shirt and knee-length, cut-off jeans, got out of the car, helped me into the back seat, and then got back behind the wheel without saying a word.

Bless him.

I curled up into the fetal position I'd been craving, resisting the urge to suck my thumb, and fell fast asleep.

When I woke up, I was in Marsh's arms.

Not a place I've ever particularly wanted to be, but at that moment, it felt like the safest place in the world. I may have nuzzled his chest with my nose.

"Big baby," he said.

I couldn't disagree with his assessment.

He placed me down on a white couch in a white living room surrounded by glass and steel and chrome. A typically sparse, modern room in another of Marsh's spare, modern condominiums.

This one I was familiar with. It was in Ghirardelli Square and looked out over the famous chocolate company and the coffee shop, FIX, that he owned, and farther onto Fisherman's Wharf and the Bay itself.

As I settled back on the couch, I realized that Marsh had carried me a ways before I woke up, which meant he had lifted almost two hundred pounds of manly flesh like it was an over-sized sack of potatoes.

He was stronger than he looked, which I knew, but still was once again impressed by.

He disappeared in the galley kitchen at the front of the room, and I closed my eyes and tried to center myself. I realized that the pain in my head had lessened a bit, but that was little comfort as it still hurt like nobody's business.

Marsh reappeared with a mug. I smelled ginger and turmeric. "Drink this," he said.

He was famous for his healing concoctions, and sometimes they even seemed to work.

I took the mug and said, "I need drugs."

He looked at me. "Drink."

I took a sip and winced. "Drugs," I repeated.

He sighed.

"My head is exploding."

He knelt on his haunches and took my face in his hands, tilting my head this way and that, examining my eyes. He got up and left me alone again.

I took more sips of the ginger brew. It started making my tummy feel a little better but did nothing for my head.

Marsh returned and opened his palm to me. In it were two oblong off-white pills.

I didn't know what they were, and I didn't care. I downed them with two gulps of the tea.

I handed the mug to Marsh, laid my head back against the couch, and closed my eyes.

Miraculously, ten minutes later, the pain, the relentless harsh pounding against my skull, lessened, then eased further, then almost dropped away. A surge of euphoria replaced it, and I was suddenly in love with the world and everyone in it, particularly my savior, Marsh Chapin.

I opened my eyes and said, "I love you, man. I really, really do."

"It won't last."

"No. You're wrong there. My love is forever. What is that shit you gave me?"

"Got it from a friend of mine, a researcher at the CDC. It's been tested, but it's not yet FDA approved. A new and supposedly non-addictive pain killer. It's not a narcotic or opioid really, or an NSAID. It's kind of an offshoot of an anti-depressant, but it works more on the body than the mind. It's a real breakthrough, according to my friend. And, judging by your reaction, you agree."

"I more than agree. Can you get me more?"

"I'll have to tell Stan that he may be wrong about it being non-addictive."

"Please," I murmured.

"You're still a little out of your mind. You have to see a concussion doc. Two blows to the head like you've absorbed in as many days is more than a little dangerous. You may even have some bleeding around your brain."

I knew he was right, but I was feeling too good to worry. "I'll have it checked out soon. But right now, we need to figure out where Jewel and Carlos might be. After what just happened, they have to be desperate to get away now. They probably figure I'm going to the police, and they must be scared out of their wits that Poe will catch up with them sooner rather than later. Can we put out alerts somehow at the airport and train station and—"

"Hold on," Marsh said. "There's a new wrinkle. Do you feel well enough to listen and make sense of it?"

"Never felt better."

He shook his head. "Right," he said, and then told me about the article that had just been published on the online version of the *Examiner*.

And what he explained completely changed my view of the case and made me realize that I was back at the beginning, right where the whole damn mess had started.

THIRTY-ONE

The story outlined how Pirate's Cove Casino had been cheated out of nearly five million dollars in a recent series of scams.

A spokesman for the casino, a man by the name of Phil Likely, a senior executive who I'd never heard of, said that investigations into the incidents were ongoing but that internal controls as well as video surveillance had been strengthened as the result of the scams and that it would be much more difficult, if not impossible, for perpetrators to hit the casino going forward.

The only thing surprising about the story, casinos always adjust immediately to any kinds of thefts, was the amount of money reported stolen.

It was at least three times the size that Poe had initially claimed when he asked me to investigate and much larger than what Bobby and Leslie claimed had been stolen. So either Jewel was lying to them or Poe had been mistaken or there was a new scam being perpetrated on top of the old one.

I thought about insurance as soon as I registered the massive dollar difference, and Marsh confirmed my suspicion moments later when he said that he'd contacted the reporter who'd written the story.

"He's been looking into Poe's life and times for a couple of years. Trying to sift through all the subterfuge, the dummy corporations, and smoke screens hiding the toxic effects. He says it's a long, slow slog and he's nowhere near where he needs to be. But it's kind of his mission. He's a young guy, maybe thinks it'll make his reputation."

"A brave guy too."

"That or just dense, although he seems pretty sharp."

If this were a South American banana republic, the reporter would probably already be dead. Although it seemed to me that America was veering closer to that sorry state with each passing day, so I feared that Poe might eventually give in to temptation.

"What's his name?"

"Nick. Nick Natalino."

"Nice."

"I thought so too. Anyway, the most interesting thing he told me that he didn't put in the story because he can't prove it is that Pirate's Cove has a loss insurance policy with a small company out of Delaware. One source, he said that it was a competitor, so only semi-reliable, claims that the loss amounts are greatly exaggerated. So Nick thinks that, right in character, Poe is trying to make lemonade out of lemons. He's trying to milk the insurance company for a big profit."

"Not too surprising." Although I'd never given it a thought before.

"No. But Nick also has a notion that this insurance company, DelMark, might possibly be at least partially owned by Poe. That way the claim is going to be pushed through without a lot of fuss or muss or close examination."

"Does he have any proof?"

"He says he's working on a couple things, but I sense it's more of an intuition on his part after the past couple years looking into Poe's affairs."

"It certainly wouldn't be a shock."

Marsh nodded.

"So," I said, "where does that leave us?"

My head was feeling much better, my mood was bordering on exuberance, but I can't say that my thoughts were all in neat and tidy order. I needed to rely on Marsh's brilliant deductive powers, which had proved more than reliable in the past.

"Well, looked at one way, nothing much has changed. We still should consider Jewel and her gang as the prime suspects, certainly in the casino scam, but also in the murders. Poe is just trying to profit from it, as he always does."

"I guess so," I said, although I felt, but couldn't explain, why I was much less sure of that notion than earlier in the day.

"Or, we could look at this new information and let it shade all that we know in a new light. Perhaps Poe was behind the whole affair. Maybe he hired Jewel to steal from his own casino, planning on a big score with the insurance company. Maybe he'd had it with his brother and decided to have him killed and, unfortunately, his daughter got caught in the wrong place at the wrong time."

I took that in, but it didn't seem right to me. I struggled mightily to tell him why.

"That doesn't make sense." I paused, covered my eyes with my fingers, rubbing my face raw, trying to clear my mind. "The casino is Poe's baby. His somewhat-legit business that supports all the other illegal activities that allowed him to purchase it in the first place. I don't think he'd jeopardize the whole thing by concocting this scam and hiring people like Jewel and her ilk who might easily spill the beans when they were questioned by the feds or the cops. It's too risky, and Poe is too careful a man."

Not half bad. I realized the drug was really doing right by me.

"Yeah, I know. I was just playing devil's advocate. Still, if I had to bet on who our murderer is, I wouldn't."

I nodded. Neither would I.

And right then I realized that it was time to join Alexandra.

THIRTY-TWO

"I'm not comfortable giving you a lot more of that pain killer. Who knows what side effects might be lurking?"

I was having my second ginger/turmeric tea, sitting on a stool at Plank's austere chrome and glass bar, feeling not half-bad, the high from the drug dimming a bit, but the pain still vanquished.

"You said that it lasts for four to six hours?"

"Supposedly, but the dosing hasn't been fully tested yet."

"Then give me four more. That'll take me through the night."

He left me alone there for a couple of minutes and returned with a tiny pill box and put it on the bar in front of me, along with another untraceable cell phone. I snatched both before he could change his mind.

"So you're going to stay after Jewel and Carlos?"

"And keeping an eye on both Matthew's gym and Fred's casino. We'll put out a watch at the airport, train and bus stations, and rental car places. We can't be sure that we have all their credit cards or any false identities. If they have a car, they could already be a hundred miles away."

"I'm not too worried about that. If they get away, it won't be for long. Jewel is smart, of that I'm sure, but if the FBI doesn't catch up with her, Poe will. Assuming he didn't hire her in the first place, which I just can't wrap my head around."

"You still have a disguise?"

"Back at Alexandra's place. I guess I could go there, but..."

"Hold on." He left the room again and returned five minutes later, holding a duplicate of the stuff I kept in my safe: mustache, driver's license, shades, plus a bottle of black hair dye.

"Poe thinks I'm dead, right?"

"That's what we hope. And this stuff," he motioned with his chin toward what he'd just placed in my hands, "should give you some cover, at least for one night."

I figured one night was all I had anyway.

From what Marsh told me, his friend in the mayor's office wasn't going to allow the false story to stand much longer. The police were going to announce their mistake by the morning, and I'd join the ranks of the undead.

Whatever advantage or surprise it afforded me had to be exploited tonight.

By tomorrow, the cops would be turning their attention toward me as the prime suspect in Bobby and Paula's murders.

THIRTY-THREE

As I crossed over from Yerba Buena Island to Treasure Island, it was a cool early evening, and I was feeling unsettled in more ways than one.

Maybe it was the itchy mustache covering my lip, or my new slicked-back black hair.

Maybe it was the suit. Marsh had had me fitted for one a couple of years back, but I'd never worn it. It was an expensive Italian-cut deal, something I would have never bought for myself, let alone deigned to wear.

I couldn't remember when I'd last worn a suit other than my high school senior prom. And that was only to please Maria Temple. At the time, I would have done just about anything for that golden-haired girl.

Marsh helped me dye my hair and then gotten me into the suit. We agreed that it was a whole new me. I looked younger—my hair was rich, lustrous, lounger-singer black. The whole getup gave me a more finished, sophisticated appearance than my normal tousled devil-may-care look.

Actually, it wasn't as bad as I'd expected. I even wondered if Alexandra would recognize me.

As I drove up Perimeter Drive, tiny Alcatraz and its behemoth sister, Angel Island, loomed, sparkling in the twilit purple waters.

And then the unmistakable contours of my destination rose up to the right of me like the giant mollusk that it had been modeled after. The resort complex, Pirate's Cove, perfectly mimicked an octopus with its sprawling tentacles possessively gripping the surrounding landscape.

Perched at water's edge was the main casino, a gigantic smoky glass round hub with eight curling steel and glass spindles extending a hundred yards to the north, south, east, and west. Two of these arms held hotel rooms coursing out over the Bay and anchored to the ocean floor by concrete hands that were topped by overhanging walkways lush with palms, fountains, Daliesque statuary, and even a couple of water slides not too far from game parlors where you could continue to lose money while getting your fresh air break from the casino.

A local comedian by the name of Kip Kato, who committed suicide a few months back, used to say that the architect, Raise Fuhlmnan, out of Hong Kong, had conceived its design after a scuba diving expedition on the heels of a bad acid trip.

It was Las Vegas kitsch transplanted to cosmopolitan San Francisco where the local media thought it was going to turn out to be a boondoggle, a massively expensive flop.

But they were wrong. Poe had his finger on the pulse of the zeitgeist, and he'd been busy printing money since the massive gambling den opened four years ago.

That's why it was hard to believe he would have concocted a risky scheme like the scam and insurance fraud that Nick Natalino was trying to prove.

But I knew that with some people, greed knew no bounds and

enough was never near enough. With Poe, if he really was guilty, I didn't think it was primarily about the money.

Although many in the media had speculated, no one could really nail down Poe's true nature and motivations. My own view, after having spent quite a bit of time in his company, was that although he was a careful and methodical man, something deep in the dark heart of him craved danger and risk.

He courted the devil and danced with the possibility of disaster and even ruin. Like most sociopaths, he hated convention and rules and the civility required for a just society.

He projected a cultured air, a taste for the finer things, a highbrow demeanor, but deep down, I knew he craved destruction and exalted in weakness and corruption of both the powerful and, especially, the weak and innocent.

Like the old Mafia dons, he'd gone to extraordinary lengths to stay out of the public eye until Pirate's Cove. The high-profile resort and casino was a departure and a big risk, or at least appeared to be.

I think it was a sign of his overweening confidence and hubris. And the fact that his reach, his influence, ran not only throughout San Francisco's criminal underworld, but extended into the highest reaches of the city's political and cultural life gave him the confidence that he could pull off the grand gesture without a hitch.

And so far, he was right.

I didn't think, like Don Corleone in *The Godfather*, that he craved legitimacy to gain respect.

Poe demanded respect. And most of the time, he had the wealth and power to get it. As long as you feared him and didn't get in his way, I don't think he gave a damn what was whispered behind his back.

I PULLED INTO ONE OF THE OCTOPUS'S TENTACLES—A TUNNEL leading directly into the underground garages beneath the casino, the place I always park when I visit the Devil's Arcade.

As I rode the glass polyhedron-shaped elevator, a near prism, up to the main casino floor, I had the feeling of being naked. Which was odd. The disguise served to make me feel conspicuous, like a donut in a flower shop.

I knew there was no reason for anyone to pay particular notice to me, other than the unseen cameras that I knew were ubiquitous here. My disguise was designed primarily to fool video surveillance. Of course, I didn't know what kind of database the camera operators were working from, but I assumed that Poe had me on a list somewhere and wanted to know whenever Max Plank paid a visit.

I couldn't be sure if the disguise would fool Poe or Angelique if I was face to face with them, but it might do the trick, or at least buy time in the meanwhile.

I'd texted Alexandra from Marsh's condo to get her room number. She'd checked into the resort in the middle of the night and had had loads of Marsh's money to play with since then.

I stepped out of the elevator and into the whirling maelstrom.

Right in the center of the massive arena-sized room was a pirate ship, a replica of the Black Pearl from *Pirates of the Caribbean*. I assumed Poe got rights from the filmmakers or Johnny Depp himself, who might very well be pleased to be associated with a modern-day pirate like Poe.

Blackjack tables, roulette wheels, and endless rows of slot machines covered the deck of the massive ship and spilled out onto other, smaller vessels nearby.

The ceiling was painted black with starburst patterns, and the light overall was romantic dinner dim. The floor was deep blue mimicking an ocean appropriate to float the Black Pearl and its attendant ships.

The jangly sound of the slots mixed with the raucous retort of people laughing, crying, shouting. The sweet stench of excess spirits underlaid the thrum of the casino itself. The punch from the place was visceral, entrancing or off-putting depending upon your turn of mind.

I always remember my first visit here with my good friend, Bo Fiddler.

Bo and I had played a few rounds of blackjack and caught a show in the lounge featuring a stoked and Hawaiian-shirt-clad Steve Miller. We'd both had more than our share of luck, an unusual circumstance in my experience. This was in the early days after the casino opened and perhaps Poe had the machines rigged to pay out more frequently then to entice customers back for a return visit sooner rather than later.

In any case, we'd met two lovely women, Katherine and Paula. Both approaching the dangerous age of forty—lifelong friends from Hoboken and Palm Beach respectively—they'd been on a weekend getaway to see if they could recapture a touch of something lost after divorces and other depredations of age. They were kind enough to spend the evening with us. I like to think they recall that night with fond smiles, and maybe a blush or two.

So, despite everything I knew about the place, I had a soft spot, a warm memory to offset the slightly icky feeling that usually accompanied my visits here.

I glanced over at the reception area to my left, which featured islands of sand, palm and coconut trees made of metal, treasure chests, babbling water fountains, comely wax wenches. The employees still wore Swashbuckler hats and pirate gear, with the added bonus, depending on your point of view, of low-cut corsets for the females.

Looking at them, my disguise paled in comparison, and I felt slightly more comfortable in the getup.

I veered around the reception and headed straight back to the bank of elevators serving the first ten floors of the hotel complex.

I KNOCKED ON ROOM NUMBER 1001 AND STEPPED BACK SO Alexandra could size me up in the little viewfinder. The hallways were long, wide, and high-ceilinged, and the floor was covered with royal red carpeting festooned with golden doubloons spewing geyser-like out the mouths of smiley-faced slot machines.

As I waited for Alexandra to open the door, I doubted myself for having risked sending her here. It suddenly seemed crazy to me. A total shot in the dark and I knew it.

Yes, Alexandra is a photo journalist and a fine investigative reporter working freelance for several media publications— primarily for one of the top British journals specializing in digging up international crimes and malfeasance.

Poe had only met her a couple of times, and only once for any length of time, when we sat at a nearby table at a fundraiser for the victims of sex trafficking, one of Alexandra's main areas of investigation. Poe surprised everyone by showing up with a five-thousand-dollar check for the cause.

He'd come over with the excuse of wanting to meet the woman who would dare date a scoundrel like me.

Alexandra had found him suave and charming, which he was. Afterward, I filled her in the other side of his character, and she was shocked at the Jekyll and Hyde nature of the beast.

Alexandra was a worldly woman, experienced with the worst acts that man committed upon his fellow humans. But true evil has no one look or definition. It's infinitely adaptable, like cancer, growing in the darkest, deepest reaches of any organism unlucky enough to accommodate it.

Nevertheless, while Alexandra was a relative novice when it

came to casino games, she knows her way around crooks and criminals, and I thought her snooping around to see what she could see while spending enough money to get the attention of higher ups in casino management might yield dividends. She was also going to see if she could get anyone to talk about the recent scams that had been in the papers.

The door opened and Alexandra, looking flustered and decidedly unlike herself in the wig and bawdy dress, clapped her hand over her mouth and said, "Wow."

I pinched my tie and wiggled my hips.

"I like the suit, not so much the mustache. The black hair is just weird."

"Take a good look because you're unlikely to see me in it again." I paused, ran my eyes lasciviously up and down her body. "But, you, my dear, make a very attractive floozy."

She frowned at me and said, "C'mon quickly, Max. Something's happened. I have to get back down to the casino in fifteen minutes."

I stepped into the room, which was a suite with two separate bedrooms, along with a kitchen and wet bar and even a hot tub tucked into a corner overlooking the Bay.

I sat down on a red stool at the bar, twirled it around once, faced her, and said, "You've already gotten an upgrade?"

"It didn't take them long to notice me. They act fast here. Can you believe that it's comped?" she said, marveling at what throwing money away can get you, at least temporarily.

"How much of Marsh's money have you spent?"

"Too much," she answered, blushing. "I think just over ten thousand dollars now."

"In less than a day. Wow."

"Wow is right. You're sure it's all right with Marsh?"

"Yes."

"Okay." She paused reflectively and said, "That photo you

texted me yesterday. The one of the woman who came to see you pretending she was Bobby's daughter?"

I nodded. I'd sent it to her almost as an afterthought, without really thinking it was serving any purpose. As soon as Portia had sent it to me, I'd forwarded it on to Alexandra.

"I think I might be friends with her," Alexandra said, giving me a veiled look.

"What?" I said.

"It was weird. I was playing at one of my usual tables and—"

I laughed.

"Hey, c'mon. You told me to pretend to be a high roller, a shark, and that's what I'm doing."

"A whale."

"Shark. Whale. Whatever. Anyway, I was at this roulette wheel, betting obscene amounts of money, and I noticed this woman at a nearby table playing blackjack. There was something about her that caught my eye. She seemed both nervous and strangely self-possessed at the same time, if that makes any sense. It didn't to me, but that's how it struck me."

She paused, thinking back on the moment, then added, "I picked up my remaining chips and stepped back from the table and opened the phone to the photo. I examined it and then the woman and couldn't determine if they were one and the same person. But I thought it was close enough to warrant my time. So I went over and sat down at her table."

I wanted to say good girl but didn't.

"After we played for a while, she took an interest in me. I was betting a hundred dollars or more per hand, so I think that got her attention. We started chatting and she told me—"

"So is it really her, Alex?" I said, hardly able to contain myself. This seemed like the impossible break that I'd been hoping for. Despite our wild speculations about how this whole thing may have started, I'd never expected to find Jewel Allen lurking here in Poe's domain.

"I don't know," she said. "Even seeing her up close, I can't be sure."

"But what do you think? Did she tell you her name?"

"Yes, we got chummy. I told her my phony alias, and she said her name was Dot. She didn't give me a last name."

"That's her," I said.

"I'm not sure. I don't want—"

"Her real name is Dorothy. Marsh confirmed that. She went by Dot as a child, according to Leslie at the gym. What are the chances that a woman who looks like her and has the same name is here at Pirate's Cove? I'm a little surprised she would use that moniker, but I guess she takes you for a local rube."

"Pardon me?" Alexandra replied, a note of irritation in your voice.

"It's absolutely perfect, honey. You're great. You've obviously played your part to the hilt, and I can't thank you enough."

Her peeved facial expression morphed into a sly smile. "Thanks," she said.

"When did you last see her?" I was trying to figure out how this jibed with the timing of my dangerous escapade at Carlos's house. I was sure the woman in the background there had to be Jewel. That had been late this morning, less than eight hours ago.

"It was early this morning."

"How early?"

"About 6 a.m. I'd been playing for a couple of hours. When I was at the blackjack table with Dot, a man came over, a pit boss I think, and whispered in my ear, offering me an upgrade to my room. I'd just dropped my bag in the one that you reserved for me on the third floor and come out to spend Marsh's money as fast as I could. After he left, Dot looked at me curiously, and I told her what he'd said. She was impressed, and I think that cemented our bond. After we played a little longer, she asked me if I wanted to have breakfast with her."

"And you did."

"Yes. At Pete's Pirate Shack. And so—"

"How long were you with her? I think I ran into Jewel around 11 a.m. so if—"

"Hold on. I haven't got to the most interesting part of all this. I think that woman who you had the run in at the Fairmount a couple of years back, the one you said was one of Poe's most dangerous people..." She paused, locked onto my eyes.

"Angelique?"

"Yes, I think maybe she dropped by our table. I don't know if it was her because you never really described her except for saying she was tall and black and a mix of another nationality, which gave her an exotic look."

"Describe her to me."

Alexandra, with her reporter's eye, gave me enough information, along with the additional obvious fact that she was right here in the casino, for me to be pretty sure that it was Angelique.

I remembered the shadowy figure outside Bobby's motel door just before I found his dead body, and an uneasy feeling again rose up in my chest.

"Did she talk to you or Dot?"

"No. She didn't. It was strange. She just kind of lurked nearby. Close enough for Dot to notice her. Soon as she did, Dot's mood changed. She went from kind of light and bubbly to very serious. The two of them exchanged a look, and Dot turned to me and said she had to go. She got up and started to leave, but turned back and asked me to meet her tonight at 7:30 at the same blackjack table if I could. Then she joined the woman, Angelique I guess, and they walked off together."

"That's incredible," I said.

What the hell was going on?

Was there really a bigger scam behind the scam pulled off by Jewel and Leslie and Carlos and the rest of the gang?

And was Poe at the heart of it?

Or was Angelique involved in some kind of rogue operation that Poe wasn't aware of? That seemed even more unlikely, especially as she was meeting with Jewel right here in Poe's house.

Angelique, by all accounts, was fiercely loyal to her boss, and the likeliest conclusion was that anything she did was in service to his interests and directed by him.

All this remarkable new information didn't change my immediate goal, which was a *tête-à-tête* with Ms. Jewel Allen.

"Amazing," I said.

"And I'm also on friendly terms with one of the pit bosses."

"I'll bet you are."

She nudged me and continued. "He bought me a drink, which was weird because I was getting free drinks offered to me to the point of annoyance. Anyway, when I was buying more chips, he coaxed me over to a little bar and we had a chat. I thought maybe he was just trying to get to know me on behalf of the casino since I was spending so much money. But it wasn't long before he asked me for a date. He's taking me to dinner in the city Friday night."

"What?" I said, my hackles raised.

"He seems like a nice guy. Good looking too," she said.

"Alex—"

"Jealous?"

"No."

"Of course not. Max Plank is an island."

"C'mon, not fair."

She sighed. "I know. But sometimes..." The corners of her mouth lowered, and she looked away. "Anyway, I'm going to stand him up. I'm working, Max. For you. I got a little chummy with him so that he'd share information. After I agreed to the date, I prodded him a bit. I asked him about the recent scams that I'd read about in the paper."

Of course that was it. Hadn't fooled me for a moment.

"I know he'll seek me out again tonight, so hopefully I'll get more, but he did mention Bobby, not by name, only as Poe's brother. He said the whole casino staff was in a tizzy because of the murders. And he mentioned how the brothers had had a falling out after it appeared that Bobby, who Poe had helped get back on his feet, had betrayed him. Paxton said that he figured the sharks who hit the casino just used Bobby and then killed him because they were afraid he might tell his brother who they were."

"Paxton?" I said.

"Yes. Stop it. Anyway, I pressed him a little more about Poe, if he had much contact with him, and he said that he did. That they met just about every day and he was one of Poe's most trusted associates."

"He was probably just trying to impress you."

"I thought that too. I think he was just sharing the gossip and rumors that always float in and around any big organization."

"In any case, Poe wouldn't be too happy with your Paxton telling a total stranger, especially a high roller like you, the company's internal, intimate affairs."

"I don't think he was looking at me as a stranger. We even shared a kiss."

"Alex!"

"On the cheek. When I left, I thought it might open him up even more later when we speak."

"You're really taking your job seriously."

"I like being a whale."

I leaned in for a kiss on her lips, but she angled her mouth away and, seeing me frown, reached up and gave me a kiss on the cheek.

"That's it? Me and Paxton only get a kiss on the cheek?"

"He's been nicer to me than you have lately."

There it was. The reason I wanted to take her to Hawaii to work things out, to make up for whatever I'd done or not done. Before this whole mess of a case careened out of control.

She reached up to caress my cheek with her fingers and said, "After this is over, we'll talk."

I nodded.

I had to shake thoughts of Paxton, the pit boss, away. He and I were only temporarily on an equal footing. That was going to change. But right now, I had to get back on point. I looked at her and said, "You've done amazing work. Really. I can't thank you enough. Now I need to have a private chat with Jewel. Do you think you can get her up to this room?"

Alexandra picked up her phone and her shoulder bag from a mirrored table. She dug in the bag until she found a small purse, snapped it open, and withdrew a thick wad of cash. "I can spend all of this and Marsh won't mind?" she asked, pursing her lips.

"Not at all." It helped to be friends with a very rich guy, although Marsh was hoping for a reward from Poe for solving the case.

That was seeming less likely by the minute.

"I'll do my best to get her up here," Alexandra said.

"Sooner rather than later, you floozy you."

The blond wig was a tad gaudy, but what really iced the cake was the short, red polka dot dress, the seamed stockings, and the high-heeled stiletto shoes. Definitely attention-getting garb. Not that Alexandra ever had much trouble catching the eye.

She smirked at me, kicked up her heel like a can-can dancer, and blew me a kiss before flouncing out of the room.

THIRTY-FOUR

As I waited impatiently in the room, my head started pounding again, the pain ratcheting back toward the unbearable.

I downed two more of Marsh's experimental pain killers and, again, they worked like a charm. In roughly ten minutes, the awful hammering inside my skull started to subside, and a euphoric feeling, an amalgam of vast love and personal invincibility, began to reshape my consciousness.

How could something this spectacularly mind-altering not be addictive, at least psychologically? I had a feeling that if the stuff ever made it through the FDA approval process, we were in for another epidemic of abuse and misuse just like with the opioid crisis.

But right then and there, I didn't care one whit.

Time passed, ever so pleasantly. I kept having to bring my mind back to the reality and importance of the moment, trying to prepare myself for what I hoped would soon be a face-to-face meeting with Jewel Allen.

I tried to worry about what was happening between Alexandra and Jewel down in the casino.

I thought about Paxton, the pit boss, and realized I didn't bear him ill will at all. It was nice that Alexandra had kissed him on the cheek. That was a pleasant feeling, and I was happy that he'd had the chance to experience it.

Around about then, I noticed the hot tub. I hadn't been in a hot tub since a little trip to Big Sur back a decade or so ago with a woman named Jennifer, who was nice enough to wash all my dirty places with a loofah sponge while we soaked.

A hot tub suddenly felt more than just a little appealing.

I stripped naked, pushed a few buttons resulting in a gurgling, bubbling froth overtaking the surface of the tub, and slipped my body into the warm water.

It felt marvelous.

I settled back with my bare ass sliding along the slippery bench seat and let my head loll back across the top of the tub. I closed my eyes, and every muscle in my body seemed to release itself from the clutches of stress and worry. I sighed as warm beads of perspiration broke out on my forehead.

Troubling thoughts strived to break through to the surface of my consciousness, but I didn't let them bother me.

The door to the hotel room opened.

"Uh-oh," I mumbled, a sudden realization that I was acting like a naughty boy.

A drunken fool. A high-as-a-kite trickster.

"Max!" Alexandra cried, when she spotted me all naked in the hot tub.

"Hi, babe," I said.

"Is this your boy—" a voice behind her said, stepping forward, her eyes doing a double take as they roamed over me.

"What the hell—" she cried, once she registered my identity.

The hair and mustache hadn't fooled her for more than a moment.

She looked at Alexandra, who had her mouth open in shock, and then back at me. "What's going on...?" Jewel started backpedaling, and I started to realize what was really going on. I scrambled to get out of the tub.

Alexandra scampered back to the room door, a step before Jewel, and placed her body back against it.

"Out of my way, bitch," Jewel hissed, dropping her handbag on the floor at her feet, plunging her hand inside to remove a small snub-nosed revolver.

I was out of the tub, standing naked, watching, trying to yank my mind out of its own personal summer of love.

As Jewel made to lift the gun, the toe of Alexandra's stiletto shoe kicked it right out of her hand. It skittered across the floor toward me and plopped into the hot tub where it sunk beneath the bubbling water.

I was overwhelmed. I yelled, "I love you, Alexandra!" and rushed to wrap my arms around Jewel, wrestling her to the ground. She screamed. I clamped my hand over her mouth, rolling on top of her.

There was no doubt that this move might be considered more than a little abusive—a wet, naked man holding down a woman against her will.

"Max," Alexandra said. "You don't have any clothes on."

She was right. As always. I was a jerk. But I stayed all naked all over Jewel feeling guilty for lots of reasons.

Jewel was mumbling obscenities into the palm of my hand, trying to wriggle away. She suddenly bit down hard, catching the edge of my right finger, clenching, twisting her head back and forth like a tiger with a fawn's neck in its jaw.

I muffled my own scream and twisted away, wrenching my hand out of Jewel's mouth, blood streaming from the wound.

A moment later, Alexandra dropped onto Jewel's chest, holding Jewel's shoulders down with her thighs.

Jewel struggled but couldn't escape, beating Alex's legs with impotent fists.

"Max," Alexandra cried, "do something. And put on some clothes."

The woman was a marvel.

A LITTLE WHILE LATER, WE WERE ALL FULLY CLOTHED, WHICH I could tell was a welcome relief to the women, sitting not-so-politely in the well-appointed living room.

I'd tied Jewel's hands together in front of her, using a torn of piece of the high-thread-count sheets I'd ripped off one of the beds. I'd settled her into a high-backed dining room chair that I'd also tied her ankles to.

Alexandra and I were seated in matching leather seats right in front of her. I was drinking copious amounts of coffee, trying to clear my head. I told Alexandra about the pain pills that Marsh had given me. She cursed me and him, but when I told her about the pain that I'd been desperate to relieve, I thought I detected a tiny dollop of sympathy flash across her face before she wiped it away.

"Jewel," I said, after downing another big dose of caffeine. I was still feeling the effects of the drug, stronger this time than when I'd taken it earlier in the day. At least I didn't feel quite like bursting into uproarious laughter as I had when I was languishing in the hot tub.

I felt cross with Jewel, tamping down the overall sense of love for all humanity that seemed to course through my veins.

She'd tried to pull a gun on the love of my life. I couldn't stand for that.

"Look at me, Jewel." Her eyes were everywhere but.

"You remember me, don't you?" She did look different than when she'd come to my boat pretending to be Bobby's daughter. Her hair was a darker color, and she had a harsher edge to her, but that could have been the circumstances bringing out the worst in her.

And by now, I was sure, the worst in her was pretty damn bad.

She looked at Alexandra. "You set me up, bitch."

Alex looked away.

"Look at me," I repeated.

She did, with venom in her eyes.

"Were you with Carlos this morning at his house when I dropped by? Did you hit me on the head?"

"Do you know where you are?" she said, lifting her bound hands up, waving them around as best she could.

She was confusing me. I studied her. She studied back, a smirk on her face, one that carried equal notes of contempt and irritation.

"What are you saying?" Alexandra asked, perhaps getting impatient with my sluggish interrogation.

I was swimming through a toxic sludge of good feeling still, but felt I was making progress.

"Guess," Jewel said, with a bitter turn of her lip.

"How are you involved with Poe?" I said.

"Wouldn't you like to know?" she answered, smiling, setting her hands down on her lap, looking self-satisfied.

She was pissing me off, messing with my Feng Shui.

"You're in trouble, Jewel. All your friends, your accomplices, have turned against you. Leslie and Earl and the others. They've told us all about the scams here. You're going to jail. Maybe if you cooperate with us now, we can help you a little, otherwise—"

"Bullshit. I'm not going to jail. I didn't steal a thing. The casino's not going to press charges against me. That's for damn sure."

I didn't like her tone of voice, but I felt a little bothersome tingle inside, afraid that her words might carry more than a modicum of truth.

Had the biggest scam been committed against Bobby and Paula? Against me? Had I wasted not only my own time, but Marsh and Alexandra's?

"Even if there's not enough evidence to get you for the casino cheats, you're on the line for the murder of Bobby and his daughter. Leslie and Earl, and even Carlos, all but told me that you pulled the trigger."

I was telling tall tales out of school but hoped she didn't know it.

"Carlos didn't tell you anything. He never would. He's crazy in love with me, just like Bobby. And Earl and Leslie, if they said anything, know nothing and can prove less." She looked down at her bound hands, shook her head, and smiled ruefully. "You're clueless, aren't you?"

That's about the worst thing you can say to a private investigator, and though I never claim to be a member in good standing in that august community, right then and there, I had the sinking feeling that she might be right.

"Only thing I don't get is the newspaper reporting that your body was found in that motel room along with Bobby and Paula. You don't look dead to me."

At least I had one up on her, one thing she couldn't figure out. It seemed like that was about all I had. It was obvious that the bother of having me declared temporarily dead had not worked at all. At least not on who we thought were the likely killers.

I struggled to determine what tack to take to get her to tell me what she knew.

"Jewel, you're going to have to—"

"No. I'm not. You've got nothing. I'm not going to say another word to you. Just wait. Do you think you can hide out here without Poe knowing it? I'd hate to be you when he finds out what you're doing."

"Tell me about Poe. Did he plan all this with you? Don't you know you can't trust him? You're the one that is—"

"Not another word," she said and pressed her lips together forcefully, signaling that she meant it.

I asked several more questions. Jewel didn't answer and didn't even look at me. We sat there in silence for an interminable length of time that probably was only a minute or two.

"Max," Alexandra said, softly. "Can I talk to you for a minute?"

She was standing just behind me, and I turned around to find her inspecting me with a concerned expression. I rose and we walked to a corner of the room, behind the now silenced hot tub, but where we could still keep our eyes on Jewel.

She leaned in close and whispered, "I don't understand what's going on."

That made two of us.

"Are you okay?" she said, searching my eyes.

"Sure," I said, feeling chastened under her probing. The drug was still playing games with my thoughts and mood, but I felt I had enough control to be aware of it.

"We're not getting anywhere," she said. "Do you think she's working for Poe? Has she been all along?"

"I don't know." I felt like I was back at the beginning, in Poe's office when he first asked me to find his brother for him. Even with all the information we'd uncovered, and the players now revealed, I felt I knew as little about what had really gone down as I did back then, at least in terms of who did what to whom and why. Of course, that had been less than forty-eight hours ago, although it seemed like half a lifetime.

Because of the drug, this didn't impact me as much as it normally would have, but I felt it and knew the trouble we were in.

I turned and looked at Jewel, who was scanning the room with mal-intent in her eyes. I followed her gaze for a moment, but couldn't see anything that might help her in any way.

"What do we do now?" She glanced up at a big clock made of glass: 8:45 p.m. "I'm supposed to meet with Paxton a little later. Do you think I should go?"

I thought about it. I doubted he could help us at all. If he was just your standard pit boss, he probably wasn't close with Poe and didn't really know what had happened.

It would be a waste of time, just like what was happening right now between me and Jewel.

While Alex and I exchanged a troubled look, Jewel broke her vow of silence, and called out, "I've got an appointment in ten minutes. If I don't show up for it, they're going to start looking for me. It won't take them long to find me. Not with all the security cameras around here. I sure wouldn't want to be either of you when they do."

I turned to her while a needling thought tried to break through a corner of my addled mind. And when it did, when the notion flashed bright and beckoning, I didn't know whether it was the drug or true enlightenment.

Either way, I figured, we were in a casino, a gambling den.

Why not roll the dice?

THIRTY-FIVE

I sat back down in front of Jewel. She cracked a smile and a triumphant flash of eye.

"Who are you meeting with?"

She smirked.

"If you tell me who and where, I'll let you go."

"No. Why should I? I told you, if I don't show up, it won't take them long to find me...or you."

"You mean Poe."

She shook her head dismissively.

"I won't follow you. I want you to tell them that I'm here. That we'll be waiting for them right here in this room."

That did the trick. "What do you mean?"

"I want Poe to know that we're here. I want to meet with him. If you agree to get the message to him and set up the meeting, I'll let you go. No strings attached."

"Really?" she asked.

"Who and where. Tell me those two things and you're free."

She looked down at her hands and wriggled her fingers. I

imagined they were getting a little numb. I'd tied the knot tight. "Angelique," she said.

I waited.

"Same place as where your girlfriend, or whatever she is, had breakfast with me. They keep a close watch on me. We have an arrangement. Once this is all over, they're going to let me go and give me some money to start over again someplace else. Far away," she murmured, and her face changed. A gleam of innocence and hope, a girlish expression for just a moment.

Now that we had an agreement, she was a font of information.

"And you believe him?" I said, assuming that all this hopeful future was a deal with Poe.

"Why shouldn't I? He's been straight with me so far. He could have really given me the business after..." Her voice trailed off. "Damn it," she muttered.

"After what?" I asked.

"That's all. I'm not going to tell you anything else. Talk to Poe. We have a deal, right?"

I nodded. "Just one thing. Call Angelique and tell her you're going to be a half-hour late."

"Why?"

"Because I said so."

"She'll wonder why. I'm supposed to be at the casino all night."

"Tell her you got a little sick. You're in the ladies' room recovering. That you'll be okay, you just need a little more time."

Jewel frowned and said, "That's crazy. But okay."

"Tell her and Poe that we're going to be right here waiting for them until 10 p.m. Tell them that after that, all bets are off. Tell them we're going to the police with everything we have."

Jewel and Angelique would be meeting at 9:30 p.m., so that wouldn't give Poe much time to think or to get here. Which I hoped would give us a teensy advantage. It also presented a problem for the good guys. I didn't know if Portia could do the thing she does so well in that narrow window of time. I was counting on the fact that she would be available at this time of night. She was obsessive about her work and, as far as I could tell, had no life outside it.

I turned to Alexandra and said, "Give her your phone and make sure she says exactly what I just told her to say and nothing more."

"Got it?" I said, giving her the sternest eye I could manage.

"Yeah," Jewel said, "I got it."

Then I went into the bedroom and made a call to Marsh.

THIRTY-SIX

After Jewel bid us adieu, Alex turned to me and repeated, "Max, are you out of your mind? That drug has made you even crazier than you already are."

That was one possibility.

Jewel had left the room, still pissed off, but with a gleam in her eye, as if she'd pulled off a coup.

Maybe she had.

As I said, we were in a gambling den, and I'd taken a risk.

And we didn't have a whole heck of a lot of time to prepare. By delaying Jewel's meeting by thirty minutes, the most I felt I could ask for, I'd improved our odds from zero to dismal.

"I need you to go, Alex," I said.

"I'm not going anywhere. Tell me the plan. Tell me you have one."

"It's going to get hairy. You have to go."

"I'm not leaving you alone here to face those people."

"I won't be alone. There isn't anything you can do to help us."

"I think I helped you with Jewel," she said and mimicked kicking Jewel's gun again.

"You were magnificent. But this is different. If all goes well, it'll just be an intense talk. That's what I expect. But don't worry, either way, I'll have Marsh covering my back."

"Still," she said.

"Go home and see Frankie. She needs you. I'll call you as soon as it's over."

With that, she stepped close to me, looked up into my eyes, and said, "Okay. But if anything happens to you, I'll never forgive you."

She touched my hand, kissed my lips, and left me alone.

It was 9:32 p.m.

There was nothing else I could do until closer to 10 p.m.

But in those final few minutes before the scheduled meeting, I'd be packing in a load of chills and thrills.

I readied myself, as I often do, by sitting on the floor in a lotus position, quieting my rioting mind.

THIRTY-SEVEN

At precisely 9:54 p.m., I opened the door of Room 1001 on the tenth floor of the Wayward Tower, the one and only high rise at the Pirate's Cove Resort Casino Complex.

I stepped out onto the lucky jackpot rug floor, and into the atrium with the elevators and stairwell, where I found the fire alarm. I flipped open the plastic cover over the red metal alarm, ignored the instructions that said, In Case of Fire, and pulled where it said, PULL.

The screaming alarm and flashing lights that followed were certainly attention getting.

I raced all the way down the ten flights of stairs to the hotel lobby with the alarm ringing in my ears threatening to kick up my headache again, but I was too amped up on adrenaline to worry.

I slowed down as soon as I hit the traffic jam around the elevators, people milling about wondering what to do in light of the possible fire.

I knew it wouldn't take the powers that be long to rule out a real fire. I assumed the fire department would show up and check things out and hoped that it would tie up Poe for a little while.

I crossed through the lobby and casino floor and exited out the wall of revolving glass to the porte cochere fronting the entrance. I walked around it and down a concrete path and then cut over a skirt of grass and entered the five-story underground garage. Across from me were several automated exit doors and a small glassed-in office that was empty.

Entering here put me on the fourth level of the garage, and I headed down, using the same route as the autos, hugging the exterior of the building. The alarm continued but was muted here. Cars passed me heading up to leave, but there weren't many, and none paid attention to my presence.

When I reached the first level, I was in the center of the complex, with the garage spread out in a large rectangle around me. I got my bearings and headed to my destination in the southeast corner.

It was quiet for the moment, and my footsteps against the concrete floor echoed in my head. My headache had returned, a pulsing, threatening hurt bomb.

I felt both stoked and enervated at the same time and knew that it was fear pushing and pulling me. My plan was nothing but a shot in the dark, with worse-than-slot-machine odds.

But I felt out of options. By tomorrow morning, I'd be facing police detectives accusing me of murder. I'd be able to beat the rap eventually, but even the thought of defending myself seemed too much to bear.

I reached the end of the building and angled south toward a small nondescript space, a step up from the garage floor, a door frame with a key-card entry.

I knocked on the door and waited.

A few seconds passed, and the door opened from the inside.

Marsh stepped out in front of me.

I followed him into a small crypt made of reinforced concrete. At the other end of the space was another door with a double security entrance: keypad and thumbprint.

Marsh punched in half a dozen numbers, placed his thumb over the reader, which flashed a green light okay, and then turned the knob and it gave way. He stepped aside to let me in in front of him.

The door led to yet another small room that contained a single elevator controlled by another key card. Marsh mumbled that this was a different key card than the one he used to access the space from the garage.

As we rode up the private elevator, I thanked my lucky stars for Marsh and his resources. After a couple of my previous run-ins with Poe, and assuming that eventually there would be more, Marsh had gotten hold of the blueprints for Pirate's Cove about a year ago and had his security people comb the plans, looking for whatever of interest they could find.

This elevator was one of the most interesting spots they found, as it was solely for the use of the owner of Pirate's Cove. A direct route to his private offices, which otherwise were manned by a phalanx of security devices and guards.

It had taken Portia a while to break into the computer systems here, but she'd eventually managed to find the servers and links that maintained the secret elevator. The door security codes were changed frequently, and Portia always got the new ones as soon as Poe and his people did. The Thumbprint keypad had been a little trickier, but she'd eventually brought it under her control. On the drive over, Marsh called Portia, and it had only taken her minutes from her home computer to add Marsh's thumbprint to Poe's, allowing him equal access.

We knew that the elevator was hardly ever used, by Poe or anyone else. It was designed and built for emergencies, in case Poe's enemies somehow managed to breach his formidable defenses and trapped him. He normally arrived and departed his lair via a helicopter using a rooftop pad.

The elevator was fast and smooth, befitting he whom it served.

In seconds, the doors slid quietly open and deposited us in Poe's private suite of offices.

THIRTY-EIGHT

After making sure we were all alone and locking the office door from the inside, we went right to work.

I'd made a lot of assumptions, and only the first one had worked out so far.

Poe wasn't here.

I assumed that Jewel had talked to Angelique, who'd talked to Poe and they, after gathering sufficient manpower depending on their turn of mind, had proceeded to room 1001 for our 10 p.m. meeting.

I also hoped that the fire alarm would delay and confuse them as would the empty room.

In the best of all possible worlds, Poe would be detained even further by having to deal with hotel employees and the fire department until all danger had passed and all was right in the Pirate's Den again.

That was a whole lot of hope and assumption and, even in this best of cases, might give us less than an hour alone here.

Of course, I couldn't be sure of Poe's plans for the night, other than that he was here as Jewel had confirmed in her chat with me.

"What precisely are we looking for, other than the camera switch and recorder?" Marsh asked, starting to open the drawers on Poe's desk.

I was looking up into a corner of the room where I spotted the tiny protruding edges of a lens embedded in the ceiling. I knew that there were a half-dozen arrayed around the room, controlled by a switch that Poe had. It wasn't connected to the rest of the network, so there was no monitoring of this space by anyone but him.

What went down in Poe's offices stayed there, unless Poe chose to record it for his own use. I didn't know if he'd turned on the cameras before he left, but we had to find the controller to make sure.

Portia couldn't access the cameras because they weren't online.

"A murder weapon," I said, perusing the trove of Edgar Allan Poe paraphernalia on various bookshelves and display cases.

"Right. Of course. But in the odd circumstance that we don't find it, what else?"

"Anything. Anything to do with Bobby or the scams at the casino or Jewel or the insurance claim regarding the thefts. Anything that might link Poe to either the scams themselves or his brother's murder."

Poe was an extraordinarily careful man. He had to be to have survived without even a single day of prison time for so long while being on the wrong side of the law as often as he was.

It was as crazy to expect incriminating evidence of any sort to be lying about here as it was to break in in the first place.

But.

No risk. No reward.

No retreat. No surrender.

I liked that one too.

Two of my rules to live by. Although I knew there was an

opposite side to those coins. You could come up tails and your risk and lack of retreat might be the end of you.

But, once in a great while, luck or fate intercedes in the most unexpected ways.

Magic is real, if rare.

I was praying for a little of the magic stuff, but I didn't dare let the secret out to Marsh, who wouldn't understand. He wasn't a believer in anything other than logic and preparation. And violence, when necessary.

He believed in his own capacities and leaving as little to chance as possible.

He knew what we were doing here was foolhardy, but he trusted me, or rather, indulged me, as he knew it was impossible to stop me once I'd decided on a course of necessary action.

"Plank," he said, holding a blue manila folder he'd retrieved from a side drawer of Poe's desk, his fingers and eyes scanning its contents.

"Here's the DelMark policy."

"Anything interesting?"

"Decidedly not. Lawyers wrote it. Indecipherable to the common man. I'm a lawyer, and it's making me grind my teeth." He folded it in half and shoved it into a pocket inside his jacket. "Later," he said.

"Any claims in there?"

"Nothing."

I moved to a large hutch, made of gleaming hardwood, beneath a bust of Edgar Allan Poe, and started opening drawers. It was the only other obvious piece of furniture in the office that might hold incriminating paperwork.

But I was open to the possibility of hidden compartments and secret doors. Of safes embedded in the floor.

After five minutes digging around in the hutch, I gave up. In one drawer, there were all sorts of financial documents and architectural drawings and newspaper clippings about the casino's history and construction.

The other two drawers were empty, save for more documents and books and memorabilia regarding Poe's Edgar obsession.

"Bingo," Marsh said. "A file on Jewel Allen."

He raised it up in his right hand, dropped it on the desk, and opened it up. He sat down in Poe's chair to read.

I waited and surveyed the room.

Where would I put a secret compartment or safe if I were a criminal mastermind?

I dropped to the floor and ran my fingers over a couple of the seams between the marble tiles. Without examining every last one of them, I couldn't be sure that there wasn't one that lifted away to reveal buried treasure.

This was Pirate's Cove, after all.

I stood back up, and my eyes roamed over the two walls that weren't made of glass. I didn't detect a seam that might signal a secret door.

I was wasting time. I moved closer to Marsh, leaned over his shoulder to look at Jewel's file.

"Nothing here that can help us really. Her prison records. Someone wrote up a bio, a history of her life of grifts and scams. There are a couple of recent photos taken from a distance, which means that maybe somebody was tracking her."

While listening to Marsh, I continued studying the room, noticing things I hadn't on the previous occasions when I'd had meetings with Poe here.

"We already know most of this. It proves that Poe was onto Jewel Allen and probably knew that she was involved in the scams. I don't know what we can do with that. Did he actually set the whole thing up for some unfathomable reason? Did he hire Jewel in the first place? That's what we need to find out." He pushed the file away, leaned down, and opened the bottom right drawer in the desk.

"Voila," Marsh said.

I looked down. The drawer was a tidy box full of electronics and wires.

Marsh reached in and clicked a switch. "Cameras are disabled. Nothing to do with the digital recorder but destroy it."

He reached in and lifted out a small rectangular metal box that looked like a Blu-ray player. He placed it on the floor.

"Let's see, what can I use..." He glanced behind him and smiled.

He grabbed a bust of Edgar Allan Poe made of stainless steel and smashed it hard against the recorder. He hit it again. And again. Its guts started spilling out.

Edgar Allan's nose broke.

The door to the office swung open, and Poe stepped into the room. My old friends, Art and Rex, loomed behind, with Jewel and Carlos, looking nervous, huddled between them.

Poe was holding a stocky gun in his right hand, pointed at the floor. Art and Rex each held a similar weapon.

Marsh placed the wounded Edgar Allan Poe in the center of the desk and removed two short-barreled, German-manufactured pistols from either side of his jacket, holding them level in each hand.

Poe looked stricken. His eyes were on the Edgar bust. I didn't know if Marsh's sacrilegious use was our biggest offense, but guessed it was something more.

He hadn't raised his gun as Art and Rex had as soon as they took notice of Marsh's twin pistols.

Poe turned his cold eyes to me. "I know you, Plank. I know what you are capable of. But I thought we had an understanding. I've forgiven your behavior more than once, knowing your code. Your relentless prerogative. I admire it. Your single-minded focus. But do you think your moral superiority excuses all?"

There was a lot he was packing into those statements, and with my brain throbbing painfully in my skull as rapidly as my heart thumping in my chest, I couldn't conjure an immediate response.

His eyes bore in on me.

"You've exceeded the limits of my patience."

"You're boring me," Marsh said, the barrels of his guns steady and aimed true for the heart of Poe. "Get to the point."

"Marsh Chapin. I'm honored that Plank brought you here. A sign of respect. An inkling that he understood the nature of his wrong, his transgression against me."

Marsh sighed. "Whoever said words will never hurt me? I'm suffering here. Give me sticks and stones."

"You'll get your wish, Marsh. We have business to attend to first. You wouldn't want to take your last breath on this earth without understanding why, would you?"

He waved his fingers and smiled, his eyes dancing with Marsh's.

"Don't claim the jackpot before the reels all fall into place." Marsh smiled right back, calm and cool as ever.

I sometimes wondered if his heart rate accelerated even a beat during these life-threatening encounters that we occasionally shared.

"Don't you worry," Poe replied. He nodded toward Art and Rex, and they marched Jewel and Carlos in and directed them to sit on a leather couch diagonal to the two solid walls of the room. Art and Rex took their places on opposite sides of the couch, hovering over the two grifters.

Carlos walked in a stilted manner, his eyes bouncing around the room. Jewel's confident exterior had vanished, but she looked more confused than frightened.

Poe moved directly toward us, toward his desk, paying no attention to Marsh's guns, and sat down in one of the two chairs angled in front. He placed his own gun down on the arm of the chair and settled back into it.

He closed his eyes and formed his fingers into a pyramid, brushing his lips. After several contemplative moments, he opened his eyes and looked at me.

"You came here because of your curiosity. Searching for answers. All you had to do was come and see me. I would have dealt with you honestly, no matter what you think. Go ahead, ask away."

I studied his placid face for a few seconds and then said, "Why did you try and hire me?"

"For exactly the reason I stated. To find my brother."

"But there was a lot more. Things you didn't tell me. Plans that would have affected me."

"Perhaps," he muttered, nodding his agreement. "But you turned me down. My original intent was true and honest. Perhaps if you had accepted, I might have told you more. Events were in a state of flux, moving rapidly."

"Bullshit."

He shook his head. "Go on."

"You sent Jewel, acting like she was Paula, Bobby's daughter, to convince me to take the case."

"True."

"Why?"

"To convince you to take the case."

"More than that." I glanced over at Jewel, who was watching the interchange with her lips parted, looking like she wanted to say something. Carlos sat ramrod straight, his hands trembling on his knees.

"Not really."

I didn't believe him.

"Was Jewel working with you from the beginning? Was all this scam just a scheme so you could bilk an insurance company?"

"My goodness, you'll believe any fairy tale you hear." He sighed. "The thefts were real. I knew nothing of Jewel, not even that she was involved with Bobby. I didn't even know she'd been hired, that he'd greased her way in here. Believe me, the people who allowed that to happen have been reprimanded, our hiring practices overhauled."

He paused, his lips curled downward. "I blame myself. I'd become a bit complacent. Allowed some in my employ to let down their guard. Allowed myself to let family ties get in the way of business."

"But I had no trouble finding Bobby. His address was literally placed in my hand. You directed me right to the place where that would happen. You knew where he was and yet you wanted me to be the one to find him. You wanted me there when he was murdered."

"I understand how you might come to those conclusions, but they're wrong. Karin was the wild card I didn't expect. We were still hunting for Bobby but had had no luck. I did try to hire you because I know how good the two of you are. I won't go into great detail, but I needed to get to the bottom of things as soon as possible." He paused, thinking, deciding how much to tell me. "There's a...kind of syndicate. On the East Coast. They're trying to hone in on some of my endeavors here in the Bay Area, to wrest away some of my most profitable ventures. And there were rumors that they've targeted me here in the casino. After Jewel's scams, it was vital for me to find out if she was working for them. If more was planned."

"I had nothing to do with any syndicate, Poe. I told you—" Jewel cried, starting to rise. Art put a hand on her shoulder and shoved her back down.

"I know, Jewel. I believe you," Poe said, without looking at her.

"It was just her and Carlos and Leslie and the rest of them. They were skilled. Talented, but stupid. The execution was fine, except for afterward. They should have had an escape plan. They needed to disappear. I would have found them all eventually, but it would have taken longer than it did. I located Jewel within three days. Unfortunately, she'd already broken with Bobby and he'd gone into hiding."

"So Karin wasn't working for you or Jewel?"

"A wild card, as I said. But I can't say that it didn't work out better than I expected. It resulted in you finding my brother faster than I could have hoped."

"So you had me followed. You had Angelique find us at the motel, and she murdered your brother and his daughter."

Poe gave me a blank stare, betraying nothing.

"And then you framed me for it. Why?"

He nodded. "I know what you're like. I knew that you'd keep pursuing the matter. That you wouldn't let go. I figured if you were a suspect, it would take you away for at least a little while, long enough for me to wrap everything up and seal it away permanently from prying eyes. I knew that you wouldn't go to jail. If there was a screwup and it looked like they were going to make it stick, I would have stepped in and cleared your name."

"Sure, Poe. I believe you." I paused, trying to parse out all that he'd said, test its degree of truthiness.

"How could you have your brother murdered like that? And his poor innocent daughter? I thought you cared for him. And I know Paula liked you; she admired you even. She told me. Bobby betrayed you, yes, but he did it because he was in love and Jewel was feeding him coke."

"Wait a minute, don't—"Jewel said.

"Shut up!" Poe's voice was full of menace, and Jewel obeyed.

"You knew his flaws. You knew his weaknesses. He was your

brother. Paula was your niece." My voice broke, and I felt the loss of those two for a moment as if they were my own kin.

Poe looked at Marsh, still standing armed and attentive beside me. Then his eyes returned to mine and he said, "I'd warned him. He knew. There is nothing I prize above loyalty. And family is the bedrock of that virtue. A disloyal family member is worse than betrayal by an outsider."

"What about Paula? She didn't do a damn thing to deserve what she got."

"That was unfortunate, but necessary, after she witnessed her father's fate."

The pain in my head had returned full force, and my stomach was roiling. I felt sick. I was sick of talking to this murderous sociopath. I wanted to unleash Marsh.

But I had one more question that I needed an answer to. "I saw Angelique leave the room. I followed her, and then I went directly back there and found Bobby's body. Was someone else in the room? Angelique couldn't have snuck back in to hit me, there wasn't time."

Poe answered simply, "Family takes care of family."

There it was.

He'd murdered his brother and niece with his own hands. Angelique had been there only as a lookout. He'd been in the room when I returned, and he'd been the one who delivered the blow to my head.

It was a huge risk on his part, but he probably thought it was his duty.

His obligation to make things right, to even the score, to make amends for the failures of his family, his own brother.

I wondered, at that moment, when he pointed the gun at Bobby, what he felt. When he sighted Paula in the crosshairs, just before he fired a bullet into her head, as she stood trembling and confused, did he feel nothing?

Had he extinguished all human feeling, sublimating them to his own selfish purposes? Or had they been stunted in the first place, never developing when he was a boy?

I didn't know and, right then, didn't care.

"Now what?" I said, feeling unsteady on my feet.

"Answered all your questions?"

I shrugged. "What about Leslie and the rest of the men that were involved?"

"Leslie," he glanced down at the Rolex watch on his wrist, "committed suicide about thirty minutes ago. A sad case. He was despondent over his lover's death and the fact that he was deeply in debt."

"What do you mean—" Jewel cried out.

"Silence," Poe said. "As for the three other gentlemen, other than Carlos here, who was quite successful playing blackjack at one of my tables, they've disappeared. Rather permanently. I doubt anything will ever be heard from any of them again."

"Oh shit," Carlos mumbled. He grabbed the couch with his hands and started to lift himself up, but Rex shoved him back down and forced the barrel of the gun against his neck.

"We're both going to disappear too. You'll never hear from us again. I did everything you asked. Carlos did too. Just give us the money you promised, and you won't ever see hide nor hair of us again." Jewel's voice pitched high, balancing on a razor's edge of hysteria.

"You want more of my money," Poe said, flatly.

"It's what you told me you were going to do, soon as everything worked out right for you. You promised. And you got most of your money back, all that I had still. Please." A muscle began trembling in her cheek. "You don't have to give us any money at all."

I looked from her panicked face back to Poe in time to see him nod his chin toward Art and Rex, who already had their guns pointed.

A moment later, two virtually simultaneous explosions rocked the room as bullets penetrated opposite sides of Jewel and Carlos's heads.

Carlos pitched sideways, a gush of blood spraying across Jewel's face as she tumbled forward onto the floor.

Marsh pedaled back, crouching into a shooting position. I ducked down behind the desk and took my own gun out of the side holster.

My heart was in my head and vice versa.

Jewel's blood-streaked, shocked-eyed face flashed over and over again in my mind. I clutched my gun. Marsh put his hand on my back and said, "Steady."

That didn't make me feel better. I took a deep breath through my nose, pictured the location of all the players, planning the next move, the right step.

"Gentlemen," Poe said. "Don't over react."

No. Wouldn't want to do that. No reason to worry.

A double murder is no reason to panic.

"You're armed. So are we. It's a standoff. Let's see if we can come to an understanding before we suffer more loss of life."

Marsh leaned in, pressing his lips against my ear. "I can take out Art and Rex with two shots. Do you think you can handle Poe?"

While I was considering that proposition, Poe said something that completely changed the equation.

"Angelique," he said, "could you bring Ms. Alexandra in?"

THIRTY-NINE

I stood up to find Alexandra in the doorway, Angelique right behind her.

Angelique had an AK-47 strapped over her shoulder and a knife at Alex's throat as she pushed her over the threshold and into the room.

Poe turned to Art and said, "Seal us in."

Art stepped over Jewel's body and moved to a table with a lamp on top of it, fronting one of the glass walls overlooking San Francisco Bay.

He knelt on the floor and reached under the table and flicked a switch.

Suddenly, the whole room shook, and solid steel walls appeared out of sheaths hidden somewhere in the room's joist structures.

The walls moved slowly, accompanied by a low hum, a funereal sound in my ears, proceeding from opposite sides of the room until they touched at the entryway, sealing tight, closing us off from the outside world.

Poe smiled. "It's kind of a safe room. Nothing can get in or out now, without my approval."

Despite his reassurance, I didn't feel safer in the slightest.

I was watching Alexandra, who was looking at Jewel and Carlos's lifeless bodies with horror on her face. Still, she seemed relatively composed despite the knife at her throat.

"So," Poe continued, "most of the loose ends have been tied up. The guilty have received their just punishment. There's just you, Plank. What to do about you."

I looked from Alexandra back to Poe, studying him, trying to figure out what he was after now. Was he afraid I was going to go to the police? What evidence did I have?

Everyone involved in the scam was dead. There were no witnesses. Marsh and I had just witnessed cold-blooded murder in the first degree. Poe and Art and Rex deserved the electric chair, but I assumed Jewel and Carlos's bodies were going to disappear and were unlikely ever to be found.

Poe was going to pay someday. I was going to do my best to see that he did.

"Don't forget about little old me," Marsh said. "I hate being ignored."

"No. You're difficult to overlook." He stepped back and brought his hand to his chin and rubbed it, like he was thinking about some perplexing problem.

"Rex, come relieve our visitors of their weapons."

"Rex," Marsh said, "I wouldn't move a muscle if I were you."

Rex stayed put, looking to Poe for help.

"Gentlemen, I believe what I have is an ace high strait, to put it in gamblers' parlance. Are you willing to forfeit this lovely woman's life right now?"

Poe nodded toward Angelique, who pressed the curved edge of her knife against Alex's throat until a small spot of blood appeared. Alexandra groaned, trying to wriggle free, but Angelique held her tight, an arm wrapped around her shoulders.

"If you hurt her—" I said.

"Your guns. On the desk."

I placed mine in the middle of the desk and looked at Marsh. He put both of his beside mine.

Rex ambled over.

"Search them," Poe said.

Rex patted us down, finding my knife in the process. He removed it from its sheath on my shin. He showed it to Poe, who nodded. He took the knife and guns with him and dumped them on the floor next to Jewel's body.

"Unfortunately, I do like Alexandra. You don't deserve her, Plank." He paused, shaking his head, affecting a sad expression. "But I feel that you need to learn a lesson. I warned you back when you broke into my home a couple of years ago that I wouldn't tolerate that kind of violation again."

The hairs on my arms and the back of my neck felt alive with electricity. The bottom was dropping out of my gut. There was only one way he could punish me profoundly without killing me.

But didn't he know what would happen if he tried that? Didn't he know he'd have to kill me anyway?

"Angelique," he said.

"Don't!" I cried.

Angelique angled her body and tightened the grip on Alex's shoulders, steadying her, quieting her struggle. She clenched her teeth and the knife quivered, then—

A blade appeared out of nowhere, wavering from where it had stuck in the side of Angelique's throat. Her hands dropped away, her own knife clattered to the floor, and she clutched her throat with both hands, blood trickling around her fingers. She stepped back unsteadily, fell to her knees, and sat on her haunches, gasping for breath.

For a long moment, nothing happened. Alexandra stood shocked still, her hands grasping her own neck, reassuring herself that it was safe and sound.

I knew Marsh had thrown the knife that he'd somehow managed to hide from Rex.

I rushed forward just as Alex was stumbling toward me, pulling her into my chest, diving to the floor with her cradled in my arms.

A bullet whizzed above my hand, shattering plaster on the wall a few feet away. Alex and I crab-crawled the couple of feet to the relative safety of the desk.

Marsh, using the desk as a shield, was firing a small snub-nosed revolver.

Bullets were flying overhead and hitting the desk, exploding splinters of wood all around us. We were trapped with only Marsh's little gun to protect us. I wasn't sure what kind it was, but it couldn't hold more than maybe eight or ten rounds. He'd fired at least six.

He fired another, and I heard a man cry out. It sounded like Art.

The firing stopped then. Rex called out, "Boss?"

I pushed Alex further behind the desk and then leaned forward around the side, back toward where Angelique had been kneeling, injured, bleeding.

Poe was kneeling over her prone body. He was holding his hand over the knife wound. I saw her chest rising and falling.

I'd never seen him look so panicked. So stricken with grief.

"Open the walls. Now!" he screamed.

Rex scurried over, scrambling, looking nervously at the desk. I put my hand on Marsh's arm. Rex snaked his hand under the table, and the steel doors began sliding open.

"Help me carry her out. Call Dr. Wiseman. Tell him to send a private ambulance. Then come back and seal the place up again the way I showed you."

Poe turned, found me watching him. "Go. The same way you came in. Now!"

Then he turned back, stood up, and he and Rex awkwardly carried the groaning Angelique out of the room.

Alexandra, Marsh, and I, not needing any further encouragement, hurried to the elevator and got the hell out.

FORTY

There couldn't have been a better place for a wedding than the middle of San Francisco Bay on Dao andMeiying's beautiful yacht, *Sweet and Sour.*

While Alexandra danced with Tommy and Meiying with Marsh, I sat at a corner table by myself.

During the ceremony, seeing Alexandra, who was, more or less, the best woman and ring holder, standing next to the couple as they stated their vows, I was overwhelmed with emotion. She looked so beautiful, and I thought again about how close I'd come to losing her that terrible night.

It turned out that no one else had died in Poe's office. Angelique had survived and fully recovered.

Whatever setup Poe had with the private doctor he had on his payroll, all of what happened that night had stayed out of the public eye.

I assumed there'd been a clean-up crew and that Jewel and Carlos's bodies were buried deep somewhere where they'd never be found, just like Leslie, whose "suicide" was reported in the paper.

Marsh had only grazed Art's shoulder with his bullet, so he'd be fine too.

Poe had called me about a week after that night to tell me about Angelique.

He actually apologized for what he'd almost done to Alexandra, claiming that the whole affair had cast him into a terrible, violent state of mind.

I didn't accept his apology. I did tell him I was glad that Angelique was going to be alright.

I still owe him one, though I don't know if I'll ever get the chance to get him to face the justice that he deserves.

Tommy and Meiying, working together, had turned all three decks of the boat into a wedding wonderland, festooned with flowers and balloons and festive nettings and streamers and other decorations beyond my powers of description.

The groom had looked resplendent in a blue tuxedo.

As had the other groom.

They were a hunky pair.

Tommy was younger, more innocent, but totally in love with Marsh.

He'd made that clear in his toast, which had Marsh blushing, not an easy feat. Marsh had been more restrained in his own little speech, but he'd made clear his affection for Tommy, who basked in the glow of it all.

Meiying left Marsh on the dance floor to go back to her job as Mistress of Ceremonies. Next up, I understood, was the cutting of the cake.

Marsh wandered over and plopped himself down beside me.

"I am happy for you, buddy. Tommy's great."

Marsh didn't respond. Not for a long time. I figured it was just more of the same. He couldn't or wouldn't acknowledge any true feelings he had.

"He's dying," Marsh said, finally.

I turned to him. "What?"

"It's in his pancreas. He's got probably only a few months. Maybe a little more, if he's lucky. Although I don't know if you'd call that luck."

"Oh, Marsh," I said.

"This," Marsh waved at the boat, all the elaborate wedding pomp and circumstance, "was his dream."

I didn't know what to say.

"His dream is me," Marsh whispered. "Can you imagine that?"

"Yes," I whispered. "I can."

"I've got to go. I think we're cutting the cake."

He put his hand on my shoulder, gripped it for a moment, then got up and left.

Frankie raced over and tumbled into my lap.

I held her tight against my chest. She mumbled against me, "This guy Nicky keeps asking me to dance."

"Good. That's good, Frankie."

"I don't know. I like him. But I don't know."

I didn't say anything to that.

She pulled back and looked into my eyes. "I can't wait for tomorrow. I've never even been on a plane."

I smiled at her. We were going to Hawaii, finally. It wasn't going to be that romantic trip I'd initially planned. Alexandra had always felt uncomfortable leaving Frankie behind.

And I was good with that now too. I was looking forward to showing the both of them my favorite places in Kauai.

I'd made sure to make amends, to give Alexandra and Frankie all the attention and time I could muster the past couple of months. They both seemed happier with me,, and I was good with that. I hadn't taken another case since then, had turned down a couple of offers.

I wasn't ready, but I knew that would change eventually.

Alexandra plopped down beside me, and Frankie moved to her, settling in her lap.

"What did you think of the wedding?"

"Beautiful," I said.

"Yeah. Wasn't it though?"

I nodded.

"I think, no matter what Marsh says, that Tommy is really good for him. I think Marsh cares more than he lets on."

I closed my eyes, but that didn't stop a tear or two from escaping.

"What's wrong?" Alexandra said.

"Nothing," I said. "I guess I'm just so happy for them."

Alexandra gave me a look, but I didn't respond.

I didn't want to spoil Tommy's dream.

ABOUT THE AUTHOR

Robert Bucchianeri is the author of the Max Plank Mystery Series along with the suspense thriller, Between a Smile and a Tear, the psychological thriller, Ransom Dreams, the rock n'roll mystery, Butcher's Moon, as well as the sunlit noir, Love Stings. He is also the author of the novella, Jet: The Fortress, an espionage thriller. Along with his wife, son, and wonder dog, Buddy, he resides, mostly, on Cape Cod.

For More Information
https://rjbucchianeri.com